Stoner Ghosts of Santa Monica

A Novel
by
Karen Karlitz

BEACON
PUBLISHING GROUP

For information, or to order additional copies,
please contact:

Beacon Publishing Group
P.O. Box 41573 Charleston, S.C. 29423
800.817.8480| beaconpublishinggroup.com

Publisher's catalog available by request.

ISBN-13: 978-1-949472-02-8

ISBN-10: 1-949472-02-7

Published in 2020. New York, NY 10001.

First Edition. Printed in the USA.

TABLE OF CONTENTS

Dedication

For my husband, Howard, who always supported my writing; for my father, Philip Wasserberger, the first and funniest man I ever knew; for my writing teacher Joe Kronsberg, who inspires writers to write; for Drs. Arun S. Singh, and Scott Genshaft; for Tish Zedalis, Jack Leslie, John Milford, Bobby Collins, Fern Wakneen, Natacha Benaim, Estelle Rattner, and Michele Kutner; and for Maya and Josh (Don't give up on your dreams). In Loving Memory of Guy Minear and Norman Chamlin.

ALSO BY KAREN KARLITZ

Baggage, a novel available on Amazon Kindle

Chapter 1
STILL HERE

I remember riding in an ambulance flat on my back, sirens blasting traffic-choked streets. I didn't know where it was headed until they unloaded me at Cedars-Sinai Hospital. I'd never arrived there by stretcher before, just came in for the routine tests. *Too young to die*, most would lament. A cliché but like others, for instance *life is too short,* true, especially when you're facing it from the other side. And, yes, there is another side. There's a lot I didn't know, like what brought me to Cedars. I had no history of the usual illnesses. In fact, I'd always considered myself lucky that way. Lucky in one area, not so much in another, which is how it often goes. Anyway, my limbs were intact so it couldn't have been one of those horrific car crashes Los Angeles inhabitants are prone to worry about.

But back to my corpse. Yeah, that's what I'd become. A corpse. I never did get around to making funeral arrangements, so I had no idea what would become of me. My future could be in an urn. The only relative I had out here, who

1

really wasn't a relative anymore, was my ex, Maxine. We weren't on the best of terms before my demise. The divorce was rough, took more years than it should have to settle everything. Problem was she never got over my indiscretions and waged a vindictive battle for several pounds of my flesh in addition to the usual spoils of a split. In my defense she didn't turn out to be the woman she pretended to be before the Tiffany diamond band (I had money back then) went on her finger. But even if Maxine continued to channel Mother Teresa, I would still be attracted to other women. It's just who I was.

We'd been married fourteen years, long enough for her to get her hooks into my worldly possessions. Her reach was exemplary. She got the house in the Hollywood Hills and I got the Malibu condo, which ultimately I had to rent out because I could no longer afford the upkeep. Those association fees and assessments can kill you. Maxine also scored the white Lexus, some cash, art, furniture and alimony. Not much in the alimony department as I hadn't been doing well for awhile. I was a writer. Hit big with a novel years before. *Herald Square* was set in Manhattan where I lived before moving west for a job in television. Came out here to write a pilot that never took off, then struggled for years, getting script doctor jobs and episode work for mostly on-their-way-out drama series. But I couldn't achieve near the success I'd had with *Herald*, though I never gave up the hope that one day I would. Yeah, if anyone asks what I've learned in this life it's that hope is what's essential.

As I said, I didn't know what brought me to this gurney parked in the hospital hallway with a white sheet draped over me neck to toes. All I know is they needed my room, and clearly I had no more use for it. I was flat on my back again staring at the ceiling. Either someone forgot to close my lids or I was able to see through them in my new incarnation. I wished there was a skylight so I could watch the California sky. In the twenty-odd years I lived out here I never tired of looking up, never took that expansive, wondrous blue for granted.

With only my mind left to amuse me I returned to pondering what got me here and had to go with the mostly likely scenario. Heart. Yeah, that had to be it. Though it never gave me any trouble before, something must have been brewing. No visitors had come by to see me yet. Maxine, who was still my emergency call contact (another thing I never got around to taking care of), was probably undergoing a cosmetic procedure or hiding after having one. She was obsessed with keeping up with those Orange County Housewives. When we were still together she'd go into a funk after watching certain episodes, usually the first one of the season when almost every housewife came back post-surgery. Her depression lifted upon discovering one of their favored physicians, and in no time she became a preferred customer of his on my dime. Claimed she did it for me, but I knew that was a load of shit.

I assumed my daughter from my first marriage didn't yet know what had happened to me. I'd hoped she'd fly in from New York when she found out. She's a good girl, thirty now, but we weren't close. Her mom, Elaine, made sure of that. There was another wife after Elaine, but that ended in a hurry. Three ex-wives and not one to cry at my grave, if that's where I end up. Maybe a few of my old girlfriends from high school and college will show up. I think some of them have good memories of me. At least I hope so. Then again, most of them still live on the East Coast. This I know from Facebook. Almost reunited with a couple of them. Actually Maxine interceded with one. Pam. I could see from the pictures she posted that she still had that same old great smile, but Maxine put the kibosh on her, went into my account and de-friended her. By the time I was free to go, Pam had remarried. Coupling, I've learned, has a hell of a lot to do with timing.

Someone rushed past me into my old room, let out a bloodcurdling shriek, then bolted back out and down the hall. "Where is he? Where the hell is Henry?" a woman screeched.

Improbable as it sounds, this gave me pains simultaneously in my chest and jaw. Another heart attack? Nope. It was Maxine's voice slicing through me like a newly sharpened meat cleaver. I wasn't happy to see her but thought she might get the ball rolling. They couldn't keep me parked in this hall indefinitely. I worried they'd forgotten I was still lying out there.

"Oh my God, is that him?" High heels clicked loudly on the linoleum, then came to a stop at my side. I didn't turn my head to look. Regardless of my feelings toward her I didn't want to freak her out, and actually I wasn't sure if I could turn my head.

"Oh my Lord, Henry. My dear, dear Henry. This can't be true." And she burst into tears. Gingerly she patted my hair, barely touching it, like I might be catching or something. "Oh, Henry, I never got the chance to tell you how much I loved you. Now it's too late." She retreated back into sobs.

I was, as you can imagine, astonished. This was inconceivable. Maxine despised me, said I ruined her life every chance she got. Guilt. She was an expert at laying it on, and to some extent I bought into it. But then I'd think of the house I handed over to her, the Picasso pen and ink, mid-century glass collection, George Nelson credenza (I better not go on with the list of spoils, the pain was accelerating), and she lost all credibility. Didn't look like such a bad life to me, especially since she had nothing before she married me, and I ended up in a one bedroom rent-controlled apartment in Beverly Hills just above the garbage and recycling bins with an excellent view into the apartment windows across the alley.

She leaned in closer and whispered, "You have nothing to worry about, Henry. Carol helped me write your obituary. Remember Carol, my therapist? She's a writer. Like you. It's running in the *Times* on Thursday. In the paper and online."

Sounded to me like the two of them were writing the obit before I fully hit the skids. In any event, it was official. I'm dead. It's going to be in the *Los Angeles Times*.

"Mrs. Davis?" a pleasant-sounding man's voice asked.

"Uh, no. I mean I was, but I'm not. I took back my maiden name after the divorce." I remember Maxine making a big point of that, saying she wanted to forget every last vestige of me, even taking back the unattractive surname of Brockenheimer. The vestiges of my house, etcetera, somehow she was able to live with.

"Is there another Mrs. Davis? Children? To help with the funeral arrangements."

"No, no Mrs. Davis, and his only child is in New York. I was so distraught when I found out about Henry, I forgot to call her. I may not be Mrs. Davis anymore, but I'm grieving all the same."

What bullshit. I would have given anything to set the record straight. I worried I'd never get to see Jennifer again. Maxine may never get around to calling her, especially if she planned to rape what was left in my apartment. She always had her eye on my Knoll cocktail table. Without Jennifer around everything would be up for grabs.

"I'm Maxine Brockenheimer now, but you can call me Maxine." I didn't have to see to picture her sly smile and suddenly perfect posture. The guy in the white coat was probably a doctor and still had some hair.

"Maxine, then. Will you be making the arrangements?"

"Uh, yeah, sure. Not ready to do that just yet. Have to look into it. How much time do I have?"

"A day, maybe two. We don't like to keep our people down there too long. Once you decide, the funeral home or crematory will come and pick up the cor…, I mean Henry."

Down there? What the hell did he mean by that? It made me feel pretty squirrelly.

"I'll do my best, doctor." There, I was right. The guy with the melodious voice was a doctor. Maxine was definitely working on a hook-up. The woman has no decency, never did. I couldn't have been gone more than a couple of hours.

"Take my card, and please give me yours. We'll stay in contact. I'll get to work on the arrangements right away."

"Come with me and I'll get you the paperwork you'll need." This guy's voice was so soothing he could have done voice-overs.

"I really appreciate your help, doctor."

I heard her high heels click down the hall, and assumed his soft soles were right beside her. She didn't even say good-bye. Recent proclamations of love aside, what could I have expected? I hate to keep piling on the clichés, but a leopard doesn't change its spots.

Oh, Lord! They were moving me, wheeling me down the damn hall at a pretty fast clip. They would never push a live one like this. The doctor must have put in the order, and now apparently I'm going *down there*. Something told me I was going to miss lying in the hall.

Man, it was freezing in there, colder than a Montreal winter's night. And dark, too. At first I could hardly make out my surroundings. My gurney came to a halt and soon after a door slammed. I thought I was alone, but then I looked around. Turned out my periphery vision had become extraordinary. The room I was in was large and scattered about were gurneys with white-sheeted lumps on top. This venue didn't look promising. I hoped someone who still had some life in him or her would get here soon to turn on the heat. I'd freeze to death if I hadn't already kicked the bucket. And my sheet was gone. I think the idiot who drove me here took it off or in his haste it flew off in a hospital corridor somewhere. My lifelong buddy must have shriveled up to nothing. It's probably a good thing I couldn't sit up and see. God damn, Maxine better not show up now. Humiliation barely describes what I was feeling. In fairness to the hospital workers, how could they have known that I knew what was going on? They were treating me like I'm dead, is all. Maybe I'd get used to this cold, like the people in Alaska.

But on top of everything, not least of which were the ghoulish bodies that surrounded me, it was boring as hell. Hmm, so that's where that cliché came from. The good news is the doctor said I wouldn't be staying long. What I wouldn't have given for a 10 milligram Ativan or better yet, an Ativan, a joint *and* a six pack of Blue Moon to pass the time. But there was no chance of getting room service on this floor.

To my left I noticed a light in the darkness. With one of my fisheyes I was able to see it was a computer screen a few feet away. If I could make my way over to it, I'd find plenty to do, maybe even start writing a new spec script. I became lost in thought thinking up a riveting opening line when I suddenly realized that I'd risen above my gurney. It was like flying, but my human body remained behind. It was too good to be true, but I swear, it's what happened. Maybe Henry Davis couldn't get back on top before he passed, but now he can hover.

Like I'd been doing it my entire life, I took to flying. I remember watching *Peter Pan* as a kid and being captivated with the thought that believing would make flying possible. I spent countless hours working on it, but it took my death for it to come to fruition. I took a spin about the room. I counted three other bodies, none of which appeared to be breathing, moving, flying or hovering. Too bad, I could have used a compatriot. I flew over to the computer. There was no chair in front of it; people probably used it on the run, maybe just to check the bodies in and out, then they'd make a fast tear back to civilization. Who could blame them?

I set myself up over the keyboard, legs floating straight out comfortably behind me, and attempted to get online. No can do. This baby had a password, and hacking was never my strong suit. Even so, I wouldn't give up. I entered numbers and letters as fast as my still nimble fingers would allow, until something tapped me on the shoulder. As you can imagine, this gave me quite a start. At first I tried to ignore it, pretend it didn't happen, chalked it up to a normal occurrence when one hovers. But then it happened again. So I flipped myself around and there was a fellow space traveler who must have flown over from a neighboring gurney. He didn't exactly have a human body, more like the outline of a body that shimmered. Picture a human-sized and human-shaped figure covered with silvery scales – no skin, blood, hair, or organs, though it did have teeth. Ghostly might explain it in short order.

"Ralph," a man's voice said.

I was too horrified to respond.

He cleared his throat. "Ralph Gordon here. Pleased to see you up and about. Most of the folks down here are, pardon the expression, deadbeats."

"Uh, Ralph, huh? How long you been here?" The scant remains of my heart thumped like a slow rap song.

"That's hard to say. Time passing is difficult to calculate after demise."

I'm thinking Ralph's family is amiss in not making the necessary arrangements to get him picked up. Possibly the poor guy doesn't have family. Or friends.

"I'm sure someone will be here for you soon," I said, trying to compensate for what I perceived may be his dearth of loved ones. Actually, I wasn't doing so well myself, having only Maxine to depend on.

"Death becomes you," Ralph said.

I found this to be an extremely inappropriate remark but didn't want to hurt Ralph's feelings. For all I knew, the guy could be a complete lunatic. "Thank you," I said and attempted a smile, which may or may not have translated to what I presumed must now be the outline of my old face.

"That's not what I mean. 'Death becomes you' is the password to get online. One of the hospital orderlies said it aloud the other day. You would think he'd be more cautious with such sensitive information, but clearly he thinks he's among the dead. Well, I mean the dead dead. Like that gentleman over there." And he pointed to a corner gurney with an extra-large lump. "He hasn't made a peep the entire time I've been here. Maybe only some of us are able to carry on after we depart."

I thought about that for a moment. Ralph could be right. But in any case, he'd miraculously given me exactly what I needed to kill some time. I entered the password and voila, I was on the hospital's homepage with access to Google and much more. I was so excited I didn't know what to do first.

Just then the door swung open. Ralph and I froze in midair. Another gurney galloped into the room. It was going so fast it was like we had front row seats at Daytona. The orderly lost control, and the gurney crash landed into the far wall. "Damn," the young hospital worker said and laughed. Ralph and I looked at one another. I wanted to clobber this guy. No respect for the dead. Putting my natural bent for justice aside, I began worrying that the moron could see us. But he walked over to the computer as if we weren't hovering above it, checked our new roommate in, and left.

"In case you're wondering, the living can't see us. At least that's been my experience thus far. I don't think I got your name."

"Henry. Henry Davis."

"Good-bye for now, Henry." Ralph flew back to his gurney and all was quiet again.

I tried not to think about what just happened. I mean none of it. I decided to concentrate on the computer. Hmm, what to do first? I considered checking out my obit but couldn't summon up the courage. I had no confidence in Maxine and her shrink's joint effort, and it was too soon to have gone live anyhow. I made several futile stabs at an opening for a new script, but nothing was coming. I was

13

blank. I headed back to my gurney to refuel my creativity.

"Good night, Henry," Ralph said from across the room.

"Night, Ralph." It was dark and quiet and cold. And for the first time in decades I fell into a deep sleep without Ambien. Seemed this passage may have been a quick fix for addiction.

The next day was full of surprises. I woke. That was the first one. Initially I wondered where the hell I was, but it didn't take long to figure out with all those corpses around. Ralph apparently was still asleep or not in the mood to socialize. I had a pretty solid idea how to begin my script. It came to me in a dream, even had a title. It was too early in the process to divulge. I've always been kind of superstitious about that stuff.

As the morning (I presumed it was morning) progressed, two more corpses were deposited in my room. I was almost certain one of them was a woman. The lumps in the area where a chest would be were extremely pronounced. This could be the work of Dr. Adelman. He was notorious for being overzealous. I knew about this kind of thing from Maxine. If this one had any spark left, things could get interesting. I must admit I prefer natural breasts but, hey, couldn't be picky in this place.

The door opened and weak light streamed into the room. The jerk from yesterday walked rapidly inside. This time he wasn't pushing a gurney. The little that was left of my adrenaline kicked in, making me almost my old nervous self. I thought he might be coming to get me, that maybe Maxine actually did what she said she was going to do, probably to impress the doctor. Crazy as it sounds, at the time I wanted to stick with the hell I knew: freezing cold room, no amenities, corpses for neighbors, one flying lunatic roommate and a dead woman who could wake at any minute. But no matter, the orderly passed me by and headed toward Ralph. Shit. I was going to miss that guy. He was the only livewire around. We could have spent the day reminiscing about our pasts, though I suspect his wasn't all that interesting. Not a party guy. Too straight, too stiff.

Yeah, I was right. He pushed Ralph to the door. As he stopped to enter something in the computer, Ralph reached out and patted me on the foot, his non-verbal way of saying goodbye. I responded in kind and shook his foot. "Good luck, Ralph," I said, taking a chance that the moron could hear. But he was preoccupied with perusing a porn site, something I would probably do myself later that today. And anyway, according to Ralph, no one can see or hear us, not with clarity anyhow.

"Bye, Henry. Have a good day," Ralph said. After a few minutes, his gurney raced out the door. I would have loved to report that orderly, but I've always believed it's bad karma to rat someone out at their job and anyway, no one would hear me if I did.

Instead of getting back to my script, I kept thinking about the new woman, if in fact she was a woman and not a man with an unusually large chest. I decided to take a fly over, as she was only two gurneys away. This was much easier than dating someone in the Valley or Marina del Rey. Even Culver City was too far in traffic. I wasn't about to get my hopes up, though. She could be a deadbeat, as Ralph called them. Deadhead might be a more accurate way to phrase it, though that would be confusing for Jerry Garcia fans. Come to think of it, it would be really cool to spend time with someone like Jerry in the morgue. There, I've said it. Morgue. No more dying in denial.

My hovering expertise fully developed, I was hanging out six feet above her gurney. It would have been rude to get any closer without introducing myself. She had blonde hair and it looked nice. Must have had it done shortly before she shoved off. Her face was pretty, though it was clear she'd had some work. Maxine would know exactly what. I guess she was in her fifties and, as I predicted, those breasts stood way too tall to be real. She looked so peaceful lying there. I didn't want to disturb her, and decided to head back to my gurney, when she said, "Is someone there?"

Thank God I hadn't gotten any closer. I wouldn't want her accusing me of anything.

"Hello," I said, looking down at her.

"Where am I? What's happened?"

I was hesitant to tell her and tried to come up with a way to ease her into the whole death thing. But the right words evaded me.

"Are you hanging up there by strings?" she asked.

"Well…no."

"It's dark in here, but I think I only see your outline. It glows."

"That always happens when I fly."

"OMG, where am I?" She thought for a moment. "Oh, no. I must have…"

She couldn't get past "have," so I finished her sentence. "Passed. We're downstairs in Cedars-Sinai," I said, avoiding the M word.

"Oh, no, that can't be. There's so much I didn't get to do, and so much money left from my last divorce settlement." She frowned and shook her head. "I bought three dresses I have to pick up at Neiman's next week. An Armani, a Versace and," she teared up, "my first Dior."

"Hey, it's not so bad. A new way of life, that's what death is. At least so far. No worries anymore. No bills, no colonoscopies, no dental appointments, no hassling at the DMV. You won't need Ambien to sleep, and no more alimony!" This last item she didn't seem so enthusiastic about. Guess I shouldn't have mentioned it. "And look, I can fly." I did a few fancy flight steps in the line of her vision hoping to put her in a better mood.

"Do you think I can do that too?"

"It took me a while, but in time, yes, I think you'll be able to."

"I've always wanted to fly. Have you ever seen *Peter Pan*?"

In that instant I was smitten. This woman was a kindred spirit *and* she was blonde. Always had a thing for blondes. I resolved to overlook the fake knockers, but just as quickly as it came, my newfound happiness imploded.

"My name's Maxine. What's yours?"

Another Maxine? Not a good omen. "Henry," I said, rapidly losing interest even though she appeared to be the only woman in this morgue.

The situation deteriorated further. Her sheet had slipped down to her waist and she was ogling her towering breasts. "What the hell am I wearing? Looks like ugly flannel pajamas. And they're avocado green. That color always makes me look washed out. Oh, now I remember! My ex-mother-in-law brought them to me in the hospital and had the nurse change me into them. One final revenge."

With each minute she seemed more and more like my Maxine, who for no reason that I could fathom had a real hate on for my mother. I said nothing. She continued with her grievances. Her voice was so shrill it could shatter the computer screen. Amazing I hadn't noticed this before. I was thoroughly turned off.

"Ah, Henry, seems like you've been here for a while. Dare I ask, how does one ring for the concierge?" she asked, with apparent distaste for the service at Cedars.

Either this woman was still under the influence of some heavy anesthesia or she was a bona fide ball breaker. I went with the latter. I'd been with enough of them to know.

"Gotta be getting back to my crypt," I said. "See you around."

"Just one more question," she said coyly.

I waited to hear what screwed-up words would emerge next from her inflated lips.

"How does my hair look?"

Jesus, really? "Great, babe. Just great."

Satisfied, she smiled and I flew off.

I was back on my back atop my gurney lamenting this turn of events, red flags flying. I decided not to make more overtures until I had time to think things through. Under the circumstances ours was fated to be a short affair, but even so, who needs the aggravation?

"Harry," she called out.

My survival instinct (surprising I still had one) kicked into gear, and I ignored her. Man, the broad couldn't even remember my name. But then she called out again in such a plaintive tone, "Harry, are you still here?" that I couldn't hold back.

"Henry," I said.

"Oh, sorry. Henry. I was wondering if you could fly upstairs and buy me a cappuccino. If I remember correctly, Starbucks has a kiosk near the lobby."

"I don't have any money. Must have left my wallet home," I said sarcastically. The nuance of my reply passed her by. Drugs or run-of-the-mill stupidity, I was having trouble deciding.

"Don't worry about it. This one's on me. Can you help me find my handbag? I'm sure it's here somewhere."

I heard her thrashing about, and against my better judgment flew over.

"I can't find it. You would think they'd have the sense to leave it by my side. Henry, darling, please take a spin down and see if it's beneath my bed."

This one wasn't playing with a full deck. "Maxine," I said, "your bag is probably in a locker somewhere upstairs. You'll reconnect with it when the, uh, people from the funeral home or crematory come to get you."

"Pleeeease, there's no need to be so graphic. Surely you can understand that I am having a meltdown." I thought she was referring to her realization of it being the end of the line, but then she continued. "I mean," and now she really ramped it up, "I DON'T KNOW WHERE MY PRADA PURSE IS!!! You must help."

"I can't fly through walls," I replied, obviously annoyed.

"Well, how was I supposed to know that? WHERE THE HELL IS MY KLONOPIN? I'm sure I stashed a couple in my pajama top, but they seem to be gone. Harry, sweetheart, could you check to see if they're in my pocket? I'm having trouble reaching all the way in."

The opportunity to forage around a woman's breast is something I'd never passed up, but I did now. "Not feeling so good myself. Think I better get back," I said, and flew off in haste.

My little bit of heaven had slithered abruptly into hell. It was like the movie *Groundhog Day*, when Bill Murray relived the same day over and over. In my version I was having the same fight with Maxine every day, which did in fact happen for roughly 13 years, only today it was a different fight with a different Maxine. I merely exchanged one ball breaker for another. Perhaps one of her ex-husbands killed her, maybe that's how she got here. It's not as if murder…a little poison or a gentle push down a scenic mountaintop…never crossed my mind with my Maxine.

I fell into a deep sleep and woke hours (minutes? days?) later. It was eerily quiet. The new Maxine and two other corpses had left the room. It was me and that extra-large lump in the corner. The more I thought about it, the more pissed I got at my ex. Apparently she hadn't done her homework, leaving me in limbo while the others except for Large Lump moved along with their deaths. So there I was, left at the altar so to speak, with too much time to contemplate where and when my final resting place would be. It was then it occurred to me that the answers to these questions might be available online. I flew over and typed in latimesobituary.com. I was nervous as hell but forged on. After some searching I came upon the obituary notices page of my D day. Before I worked up the nerve to check mine out, I read the others, something I had been doing every morning the last few years. It's not like I actually wanted to read them, but whenever I reached those pages, I just couldn't turn away.

Is it unethical, I wonder, for people to lie in writing this stuff? All these accomplishments and lofty ideals, are they fudged the same as resumes and dating site profiles? Reading about my comrades in death, I feel as though my life's work and principles pale in comparison. No way can I compete. Truth is, if I could the *Times*

22

would have assigned someone to write my obit. That's when you know you've really made it. Were so many mere mortals as kind, generous, creative, intelligent, adventurous, courageous, spiritual, multi-talented, inspiring, selfless, beautiful, loving and beloved as their obits suggest? And what about that endless list of loved ones many people leave behind? Now that is a feat to be truly envied, and at more than a hundred bucks a column inch, costs a pretty penny.

It was then I noticed my photo. It was small, but no doubt about it, it was me. My name was underneath and I looked like shit. I was fairly certain it was one of the shots Maxine took following our final divorce settlement hearing. Gloating as she turned her camera on me, she said, "For posterity." Then she cackled. I'd been plundered and pillaged like a Vietnamese village, and the air conditioning system in the courthouse had been on the fritz all day to boot. Not a good look. No, this particular snapshot was chosen by Maxine with considerable thought. No woman on Facebook (Maxine will definitely post the news of my death and this picture on her page) could possibly care about me now, and with that image fresh in their minds, what would they write on Legacy.com? "Poor Henry. He used to be so handsome." Increasing my humiliation, my obit is one of the shortest on the page, and Maxine didn't have the decency to lie, not even a little.

But it got worse. How the hell did she come up with: "In keeping with Henry's final wishes, there will be no funeral services. Instead friends and associates are invited to a celebration of Henry Davis' life Monday, 9 a.m., at Nate 'n Al's deli on Beverly Drive. Henry's ashes, a series of photos" (I trembled at the thought of them), "and signed copies of *Hereld Square* available for purchase will be displayed."

First off, the idiot woman couldn't get the spelling of my book right. And secondly, I never said any such thing about not wanting a funeral. In fact, I had fantasized plenty about being buried with great fanfare in Westwood Village Memorial Park near Truman Capote, John Cassavetes or Marilyn Monroe ever since wandering the grounds there several years back. But all this came as no surprise; I'd surely end up in an urn. The cost of burial is far higher than cremation, and Maxine knew how to watch the bottom line, especially since she'd no doubt wage an epic battle to collect whatever I'd left over. Too late now, I remembered that I never changed the beneficiary on my worldly goods, with the exception of the condo. Irv Goldstein, my lawyer, took care of putting that in Jennifer's name after the split. He advised me to do the same with my money market funds, stocks and personal belongings, but I never got around to it. So Maxine may also get possession of the urn

(Tupperware? Cookie jar?) she stuffs me in. Now that was one bloody frightening thought. Too bad I didn't try to find the Klonopin in dead Maxine's pajama top. I didn't remember ever needing drugs this much.

The door slammed. I rushed back to my gurney and wondered if they were coming for me or the lump. The guy who entered the room wasn't the usual jerk. It could have been my imagination, but this one looked like a waiter named Ernie who'd been working at Nate 'n Al since the '80s. He started pushing me to the door. If he loads me onto one of their delivery trucks, I'd know it's Ernie for sure.

* * *

Turns out you can go home again. At least I could. Maxine put my urn on the fireplace mantel shoved behind a terrific Murano vase I bought at the Rose Bowl years ago, in the living room of the house I loved and lost in the hills. I didn't know how long I'd been here or how long I'd stay. Time, as I've been told, has no meaning in death. Maxine hadn't paid much attention to me, but every now and then she would stalk over to the mantle and threaten to open the urn (yeah, she sprang for one) onto Sunset Boulevard. This generally occurred after some guy blew her off. It didn't take them long these days to realize they should make a run for it. I wasn't worried, though. Death was good. I was able to fly around the house. She hadn't caught me at it, so like Ralph surmised, she didn't see me. I still couldn't fly through walls, although Olivia, the woman ahead of me at the crematorium, claimed to be able to. Whether she was delusional, a liar or could do something I couldn't, I never did find out.

Maxine kept her bedroom door shut, sometimes even locked, but trust me, I wasn't the least bit interested in what went on in there. A bucketful of Viagra couldn't have gotten me inside that pile of fire ants.

Using a Hotmail account my housemate knew nothing about, I wrote and submitted when she wasn't home. I stuck to short stories. They lend themselves to making fast retreats from the keyboard. And when she left the back door open, I went for a spin in the yard. For some reason, maybe lack of practice, I couldn't fly past the property line, but there was no need to. My house had an awesome city view. I often enjoyed floating down onto a lounge by the pool. Sunlight caught the rippling aqua water as I laid back and gazed up at that big blue cloudless sky, watched the palm fronds dance, and dug the velvet breeze. A beer and a joint would have been nice but, man, I knew I had it made.

If you wonder what I thought was important after all I'd been through, for me it still came down to hope. Like that old song from

26

"Damn Yankees" says, you gotta have it. Oh, and one more thing. Heart. It's true enough to be a cliché. Yeah, "you gotta have heart." No pun intended.

Chapter Two
DEAD AND WELL

I didn't know what the hell was happening. I started to shake like a plastic reindeer stuck inside a snow globe in the hands of a winter blizzard fanatic. Oh, man, no. I worried this was the Big One every Californian pushed to the back of their minds instead of hopping onto the next moving truck. When I'd flown into my urn the night before to catch some R & R all was well, but now it was pitch black and I couldn't get out. Access in and out of my urn had never been a problem before. I felt a full-blown anxiety attack coming on when the shaking stopped after one last heart-stopping (if I had one) thud. I seemed to have landed. Somewhere.

I was able to see now. Light filtered through the cracks of what appeared to be the cardboard box I was stuffed into, crammed between a host of household objects covered in bubble wrap: my favorite Murano vase, a green ceramic woman circa 1950, a Richard Wright sugar and creamer. There was probably more, although I couldn't see what, and that anxiety attack grew in velocity as the box got walloped, first on top, then on the side. Then silence, followed by intermittent thumps and crashes. A man said, "Put it over there," "Don't break anything. She looks like she'd kill us," and "This woman is some piece of work." It was safe to assume he was referring to Maxine. Finally, doors slammed and whatever vehicle I was in started moving slowly, then speeded up. I had no idea where the hell we were off to.

All had been well in my house in the hills. It still irked me to say this and always will, but it was no longer mine; it was you know whose. And now there was a barrage of violence. Frankly I was scared to death – good thing I was dead already. My guess was that Maxine was moving, but I'd have to wait to see.

I was still a novice at this death thing, but so far it hadn't been all that different from life. Except, FYI, although no one alive could see me, dogs sometimes barked at me, and once a psychotic cat circled me like a bird she contemplated eating, hissing and baring her sharp little teeth without letup. Sweetie (yes, that was the feline's name) wouldn't stop until Maxine's neurotic friend Angelina took her crazy cat home. Not long after, Maxine and Angelina had a falling out over some guy who apparently preferred Angelina, so I no longer had to deal with that deranged animal. Good thing, too, the little shit could have blown my cover. But enough of that. Back to the facts of life after death: I no longer had to work, pay bills, renew my driver's license, worry about my credit score, buy insurance or go to the gym, and I didn't get entangled in human relationships and foibles. You could say after almost sixty years of living at last I was my own man. But I couldn't fly through walls, or cardboard boxes for that matter. I was a captive audience until someone, most likely Maxine, unpacked me. And since she was no maven in the housekeeping department beyond having a ready list of cleaning services and restaurants that deliver, I could be holed up in this box for months, years even. I forced myself to focus on the little I remembered from the teachings of Deepak Chopra. Maxine dragged me to his lectures a couple of times when our marriage was tanking. A long tank, come to think of it: I'd say thirteen of the fourteen years we hung in. She was still into all that meditation crap, but from what I could see, and since I lived with her it was more than I cared to, it hadn't helped her. Not a bit. Still, I blew through some mantras, and after a fitful start fell into a dead slumber.

* * *

I got out of the box. Freed at last. I didn't know how long I was in captivity, but at that point Maxine had me locked in a tight fist grip, her newly-sharpened, ink-black polished nails

30

looking more like weapons than ever. She walked me around rooms I'd never seen before. It beat being locked in a box, but not by much. "Where should I put the bastard?" she said aloud, skulking from room to room.

There didn't seem to be much space in this place. I guessed it was a two bedroom/two bath., a big step down from the mid-century ranch I bought with the royalties from my novel. I loved that house, but clearly Maxine had run amuck financially (no surprise there) and had to sell it. It might have even been foreclosed on, which broke my heart. But like they say, you can't take it with you.

She opened a closet in a small bedroom. "Welcome home, Henry," she said sarcastically. She slammed my urn down on the shelf over the clothes bar, then stood back to look at me. Silently I waited, hoping she had a change of heart. The apartment is depressing enough, but this closet was a killer. She started walking away, then turned back around and said, "Better not leave him there." I was thinking that she was thinking I deserved an important, more prominent spot, when she said, "This won't work. I'm so short on closet space." She whisked me up and hurried into a small dinette. There were three built-in shelves on the wall, and she plopped me on the top one. Gazing through a nearby window between leafy trees I saw cars going by, then a

Big Blue Bus. I figured I was in a Santa Monica rental; I lived there years back when I first came to L.A. and took the Blue Bus Line from time to time. It was a long way from the house with a pool and city view, but this neighborhood's cool. I just hoped she wouldn't move me back into a closet, or worse, stash me in a kitchen cabinet.

Maxine had gone out and I was free to roam the premises. Even though she couldn't see me, I kept a low profile when she was around. I never knew when I might bump into something and bring attention to myself. Like the time I accidentally flew into the fake Tiffany lamp with the crystals hanging from its shade. A terrible lamp: her purchase, not mine. It wobbled, but thank God it didn't hurtle to the floor, and the crystals swayed and tinkled. This freaked her out. Now don't get the wrong idea, it's been a long time since I cared about her feelings, but if she gets wind of something supernatural going on she could bring in ghost busters, and then who knows what would become of me. It's especially essential to keep off the computer when she's home. Nothing like seeing keys move up and down by themselves to make her want to Google search the best ghost busting companies in Los Angeles. I didn't have much faith in their ability to track me or my fellow deceased fliers down, but you can never know when someone who actually knows what they're doing will turn up.

It felt good to spread my wings again (just kidding, I don't have wings), and fly around my new digs. Man, that box was a bummer. Like I thought, the apartment was a two bedroom/two bath. There was no fireplace in the living room, hence no mantel for me, but there was a balcony and luckily Maxine left the slider open. I flitted outside for a look and alighted on the railing. I swore this could be the *Melrose Place* set. Years ago I watched the show with Maxine as part of our therapist-advised togetherness effort. I complained to her that the show was an insult to anyone's intelligence, but truth be told, I loved it. Never missed an episode, even in reruns. Secretly I thought about how cool it would be to live in a place like that.

Looking down from the balcony I saw two beautiful, young blondes on lounges beside the pool, while a dead ringer for Dr. Michael Mancini barbecued burgers on a grill in a small, grassy area. It was sunny and warm and the palm trees rustled gently in the breeze. Man, this place was paradise. I fully expected Amanda (I've always had a thing for Heather Locklear) or Allison to show up any minute. I'd died and gone to *Melrose Place*. But then I started worrying. Even death couldn't cure me of that. First it was about the prospect of crazy Kimberly living in the building. She and Maxine seemed like kindred spirits and would likely be best friends. Then the thought that I was incapable of making it down to the pool took root. While I considered myself an excellent flier, I couldn't fly beyond certain parameters. In my house, I couldn't go further than the backyard. Maxine's new apartment was on the second floor. I hesitated. I'd yet to attempt a mission this daring, but this pool scene was too alluring to pass up. I gave myself a "can do" pep talk, the kind you see on late night television infomercials, looked at the blondes for inspiration, and took off. Without a hitch, I zipped over to the lounge next to the blonde wearing the smaller bikini. I stretched out on my side leaning on my elbow.

"He's not going to text me back. I know it," said the blonde closest to me. She looked like she was about to cry.

"Stop looking at your phone every two minutes, Emily. It only makes waiting worse."

Emily checked her phone, then passed it over for her friend to see. "I told you," she said.

"Chill, will you?"

Emily sighed, then pulled a joint from her beach bag. She lit up. "Want a hit? It's really good medical."

"Sure. No auditions this afternoon. How about you?" She took two tokes, then passed it back to Emily.

"Free. As a bird." Emily inhaled deeply, then tossed her phone into her bag.

I hovered over them, attempting to breathe in as much secondhand smoke as I could. I wasn't sure I was getting high; I hadn't had any weed since my demise. But suddenly I was feeling pretty damn good, and hummed a few bars from the song, *"Heaven, I'm in Heaven,"* as I made my way back to my lounge. This place turned out to be even cooler than my house which didn't have many babes around. Maxine might be considered hot if you're into extensive plastic surgery, but she usually didn't surround herself with good-looking friends. Couldn't handle competition. I nodded off, and when I woke, the blondes were gone. I flew back upstairs in a hurry. I didn't want to be locked out on the balcony, but the coast was clear, Maxine hadn't returned. This glorious place was mine, all mine. At least for a while.

I flew from room to room and looked out every window. Maxine had the smarts to get an apartment with views on three sides. From the south-facing window in the living room I saw a busy, wider street a block away. I thought it might be Wilshire Boulevard, but I didn't think I'd be able to fly that far. Daydreaming about future action at the pool and with an idea for a new short story percolating, I returned to my urn. As I was settling in, a door slammed. Maxine entered the kitchen and dropped a couple of Ralphs bags on the white tile counter. "What a dump," she said, as she put away the groceries. Well, at least one of us was happy.

* * *

Maxine got a job. Her finances must have been royally screwed for her to do something that drastic. Then again, the alimony dried up when I died, and she never was one to save for a rainy day. I was shocked to see Ralphs bags. She was definitely a Gelson's or Whole Foods woman. I couldn't imagine what she was doing to earn a living. She had no skills I knew of, at least none that were legal. She probably could make a pretty decent living doing *that*; I admit it's what hooked me. But Maxine would never give head professionally. She was, however, desperately trying to nab a wealthy guy, and no doubt this talent of hers was front and center in her arsenal of female weaponry. This was just an educated assumption; like I said, I stayed out of her bedroom when she was in it. But so far she had nothing to show for it, no boyfriend, no perks from a rich male, and certainly no ring. The good news was she was out every day by eight and didn't get back until at least six. I became a regular at the pool. It wasn't *Melrose Place,* but it was a remarkable facsimile. One particular day was especially exciting. Through the dinette window I saw a United Van Lines truck parked in front of the building. Someone was moving into the vacant apartment next door to us.

I watched as two large men hauled boxes and furniture out of the truck and into our building, then realized I would see more from their balcony, which was separated from ours by a low stucco wall. I made the easy trip over. Their slider was closed but the blinds were open, giving me an excellent view of the bedroom. I was pleased to see the new occupant had excellent taste in furniture. Looked like expensive stuff. Whoever was moving in most likely hit the money skids too. I wondered if it was a man or a woman or a couple of some sort. I wasn't in suspense long.

"The bed goes on the right," a woman said. She followed closely behind the movers as they all entered the room. She motioned to the wall adjacent to Maxine's bedroom opposite a Heyward Wakefield dresser. I saw her from the side but couldn't get a good look at her face. Next the men dropped off several large wardrobe boxes, and the woman began hanging clothes in the small walk-in closet. Now I could see her from behind. She had blonde hair and a great ass. Maxine wasn't going to like this, not unless her face didn't match the rest of her. I felt content to watch and wait for the reveal. It was another beautiful day, and the westerly sun shone into her new bedroom like a welcoming spirit.

"Miss Pam," a man's voice from another room shouted. "We're ready to go. Everything's off the truck."

She hurried out of the room, as I turned to watch Michael Mancini's double doing laps. He was the only one at the pool. Later would be different. On weekends it was packed down there, and people stayed late into the night. Maxine complained a lot about the noise, mumbling how inconsiderate her "renter neighbors" were. Sometimes she slept on the living room couch because that room didn't face the pool. I heard her tell her friends that at forty-six she was too old to do the pool scene, and considering her thighs, she was right. The pool goers ranged from their early twenties to early thirties, except for a couple of fifty something men who hung out there for obvious reasons. I'd seen older people in the building, some way older. Probably original tenants who had been here since the building went up. You could find them in the laundry room, throwing out their garbage or getting their mail, but never at the pool. Except for Sylvia. She did early morning laps every day except when it rained, then hurried back to her apartment wrapped in a long white terry robe. Maxine would be wise to follow her example.

A door slammed. The movers were gone. The woman walked into the bedroom, sat on the unmade bed and stared sadly out the window.

There was a view of the pool from this vantage point, but I don't think she saw it; she seemed light-years away. I studied her face. There was something strangely familiar about it. I knew this face but couldn't place it. College? The New York bar scene when I still lived there? Here in L.A.? She was more than someone I merely nodded to in passing. I'd figure it out, but meanwhile I would go to the pool. Emily had just got there and brought some new friends with her.

I ended up hanging at a patio table with Larry and Greg, the two older guys. They were in a heated discussion about muscle cars, a subject I knew nothing about and didn't care to learn, but they were passing around some good weed, and I had a pretty nice buzz going. But something was gnawing at me. It was that woman. Where did I know her from? It was like when you can't remember the name of a book or movie: it drives you nuts. Smartphones were great for stuff like that, but a smartphone couldn't tell me who my new neighbor was. In my semi-stoned state I decided to take another look in her window. I figured that should jar my clouded memory. I walked serenely up the staircase. When I got to the top, Maxine was standing in the outside walkway, keys in hand, talking with the new woman. I hurried over, most of my mellowness dissipating along the way.

"I suppose it will have to do for now," Maxine was saying bitterly. "Since I moved in, I've got one foot out the door."

"Is it really that bad?" the woman asked.

"I've lived in far better places," Maxine said smugly. "I had a house in the Hollywood Hills. A beautiful house with a pool and a view to die for."

"My sister found me this apartment. She lives on 9th Street."

"You're from New York."

"My accent gave me away?"

Maxine laughed. "Impossible to miss. Yours is the kind you never lose. You know, you look familiar."

"I visit my sister here a few times a year."

"No, I don't think it's that." Maxine stared at her. My ex never had any shame. Was she checking her face for signs of surgery, prospecting for flaws or both? "What's your name?"

"Pam." She looked beautiful when she smiled, though why she was smiling at Maxine was a mystery to me. I rooted for Pam to go back into her apartment.

But then I was staring at her too. It was her voice. I knew this voice. Then it hit me right where my heart once was. I concentrated so intently on her face that an overlay of forty years lifted, and I could see her now as she was then.

This woman was Pam. Yeah, yeah, sure I was stoned, but I was certain this wasn't just any Pam. This was *Pam*, my college girlfriend, the proverbial one who got away. She left me because I couldn't stop screwing around, said I hurt her once too often. We almost hooked up again. On Facebook. Maxine and I were having problems (nothing new there) and Pam was going through a divorce. When Maxine got wind of our online reunion she went postal. Screaming like a woman possessed, she got into my account and defriended Pam. She told me we owed it to ourselves to give our marriage another try, then acted like Mother Teresa again. By the time she reverted back to her usual miserable self, I heard Pam had remarried. I lost her twice.

"What brings you out here?"

"My sister. She always wanted me to live near her, now especially. My husband died in November."

"Sorry," Maxine said, with no apparent sympathy. "Mine died too. Only I skipped the mourning. We'd already divorced. He screwed around. A lot. The lying piece of shit just couldn't keep it zipped."

"I had that problem with someone once, but not with Edward. It was back in college."

"Where'd you go?"

"NYU. It was a long time ago."

"Funny, that's where my ex went. Wait a minute. You're not Pam Singer, are you?"

"Not anymore, but I was."

"You've got to be kidding. Henry hooked up with you on Facebook. While we were married. And I know for a fact that you knew he was married to me. That's where I know you from." Maxine was ready to blow. The hair on top of her head stood straight up giving her a crazed porcupine look, her face turned red verging on purple, and she was breathing hard. This wasn't the first time I'd seen this transformation, not by a long shot.

"Henry Davis is dead?" Pam asked, clearly upset.

"Yeah. The bastard died two years ago."

"I'm so sorry to hear that."

"You're upset," she said sarcastically. Maxine looked like she was about to leap over to Pam, get her in a choke hold and pummel her to the ground. Pam was too distraught to notice.

"Well, we…"

Pam still cared about me! I often wondered if she did. I never stopped thinking about her.

"Wait here. I have something for you," Maxine said, and rushed into her apartment. I got ready to freak Maxine out with one of my best ghostly moves if she returned with a knife or a frying pan. She'd come at me with both. Seconds later she was back clutching my urn. I was glad I wasn't in it.

"Here. Take him. He's all yours." She thrust the urn at Pam with so much force that if Pam didn't catch it, it would have smashed against the building across the street, scattering my ashes over 4th Street.

"But you were his wife. Don't you want…"

Maxine cut her off. "I've been dying to dump the scumbag since I ended up with his ashes. I don't know why I kept them this long. I suppose it's because I'm such a good person." Experience had taught me to tread cautiously around anyone who claimed to be a good person.

Maxine was at the hyperventilation stage now. The only thing that would bring her down from this were a couple of Valium and several tumblers of red wine. "I hope you two are very happy," she screeched, then stomped into her apartment, slamming the door behind her.

Pam was left in the walkway holding my urn. Happily I hopped in.

So that's how I ended up where I should have been all along. My urn sat on top of her dresser with a view of the pool, and my girl shared my room. She talked to me a lot, and sometimes while she slept I entered into her dreams. Yes, dead people can do this. The next morning she'd tell me about the dream she had.

"It was like you were really there, Henry," she'd say, with her beautiful smile. Man, I was lucky. You know what they say, the third time's the charm.

Chapter Three
FREQUENT FLIERS

I was flying right behind Pam as she made her way to the laundry room, a dismal place with three washers, three dryers, and a wall fan clogged with black soot that was never turned on. A perennial puddle lurked in the middle of the dirty cement floor separating the washers from the dryers, making all laundry transfers challenging.

Pam opened the door, and as we entered I just missed crashing into a kindred spirit, the first I'd encountered in the building. Actually, I hadn't seen any fellow deceased fliers since I was at the crematory.

"About time you got here," he said. Not an auspicious way to greet a comrade, but he was smiling so I figured he wasn't really angry. His outline shimmered in the fluorescent light beaming down from the ceiling. He was short for a man, thin and wiry, and had a captivating grin.

"Couldn't get through the door, right?" I said, as Pam loaded two washers with a week's worth of stuff. The dead, contrary to what Hollywood would have you believe, must wait for an opening to proceed in our travels.

"I've been holed up in here since yesterday. Don't the people in this building wash their clothes?" He flitted back and forth nervously.

"You're in this building?" I asked.

"In 105. What about you?"

"We're in 202."

"Ah, penthouse people. Who's the chick?"

"You wouldn't believe it if I told you."

"Try me. But don't take all day. I want to get back to my urn."

"She's my old girlfriend, Pam." And I proceeded to tell him the saga of how my urn ended up on Pam's dresser.

"Some trip," he said, flying nervously around the doorway.

"I'm Henry. Henry Davis. What's your name?"

"Jerry."

"Ever hang out at the pool, Jerry?"

"Nah. Never was much of a pool kind of guy."

"Pam's going to work after she's finished here. Come by and check it out."

"Maybe. Gotta get going," Jerry said, hastily flying out the door.

Later that day at the pool, the place was filling up fast, typical for a Friday. I sat on top of a patio table between Larry and Greg. Larry's never been married; Greg did the deed four times but nothing stuck. They were both in sales. Larry sold used cars down on Lincoln Boulevard and Greg sold insurance. They shared a two bedroom on the first floor facing the pool, a prime location for catching the action. These guys always had the best marijuana, providing me a free and splendid contact high whenever I was near them. I was sitting there, sun shining, blue skies bluer than blue, and feeling no pain, when Jerry flew over.

"Hey, Jerry. Glad you could make it."

"Ah, I don't know."

"You into weed?"

"Never cared for gardening. Don't have the patience for it. My wife, that was her domain. We had a house in Mar Vista. She grew beautiful roses."

"I'm not talking about roses, Jerry. Weed, man. You know, pot, marijuana, grass."

"Oh, that. Never tried the stuff. Hardly even drank. Leslie, too. Not that I care what anyone else does."

"Sit next to me. And breathe. Deep."

"I don't think so."

"It's not going to kill you."

"Apparently."

"Come on, it's Friday."

"Okay, okay, I'll sit. But not for long."

I sat atop the white plastic patio table, legs dangling over the edge, swinging like the boy I once was. Jerry was stiff (pardon the expression). His legs hung straight down like he was posing for a 1950s class picture. A soft breeze stirred the palm fronds above us. Larry and Greg passed the joint back and forth. Smoke filled the air.

"Man, am I twisted," I said.

"Henry, nothing's happening. Nada. Zip. Not that it matters."

"Give it time."

The pool party was in full swing. Picture a classic shoot of *Melrose Place,* but without Heather Locklear (a serious handicap). At the risk of sounding like a dirty old man, most of the chicks were awesome, and they outnumbered the guys about two to one. The women liked to bring their friends over, but the guys for obvious reasons almost never did. Why muck up their advantage? Every lounge was taken, and the standing-room only people filled the space that was left. It was still light out, but this would go on long into the night. I spotted Maxine standing on her second-floor terrace, her face cloaked with the disdain she felt for her neighbors, for the world actually. She clutched a jumbo goblet of red wine. If looks could kill, as they say, there

48

would have been a poolside slaughter. I quickly switched my focus to Jerry, who appeared to be wasted.

"Henry? That's your name, right? Jesus, I don't know what's going on, but maybe that's a good thing. My scales are tingling, and I can't think of a single thing to worry about."

"You're stoned, Jerry. Relax and enjoy. It's not going to last."

"Larry and Greg live next door to me. I always thought they were jerks. Now I'm smoking marijuana with them. Death takes us on some strange turns. Pretty funny, huh?" and he laughed uncontrollably. I smiled, remembering laughing jags happening to me in my early smoking years.

"So this is what I've been missing. Reminds me of something. What the...yeah, I know. The time I took two Xanax. This is better."

"Stick with me Jerry, and I'll turn you into a stoner. And anyway, we're the only two spirits in the building."

"That we know of, Henry." Jerry winked and burst out laughing.

* * *

"Are you in your wife's apartment?" I asked. Jerry and I were sitting on cheap green plastic chairs on his patio. Taking discrete peeks through his glass sliders, I saw whoever it was had no taste. The furniture was ugly old, not vintage old. The pool was deserted except for Sylvia doing laps.

Jerry fidgeted in his chair. The guy never stopped moving. He mumbled something I couldn't make out.

"What did you say?"

Still speaking in an unusually low voice for him, he said, "She, uh, she," he gritted his teeth, "she left me. Years ago. Took her rose bushes with her. She ran off with our pharmacist. Moved to Sherman Oaks. Guess I should have picked up my prescriptions myself."

"Sorry, man. Any kids?"

"Nah. Claimed she didn't want any. Then she went and had a couple with Ted. I never saw them."

"Who would want to?"

"Yeah, who would? I never got over it. Couldn't bring myself to date or anything. It was a trust thing."

"When two people get together usually one does the screwing and the other one gets screwed over."

"Which were you, Henry?"

"The screwer. Couldn't keep it in my pants. But in the end my last wife, Maxine, who in my defense was a bona fide psychopath, got her revenge. Big time. She killed me in the settlement. I went from living large to reading grocery circulars and clipping coupons. Lived on chicken when it hit 99 cents a pound. She said I had it coming."

"A player, huh?"

"It had its moments." I couldn't keep the smirk off my face remembering the good times. Luckily Jerry, who was depressed as hell, wasn't looking at me. I never should have brought up the wife.

"I was always better with the horses than the ladies. Loved the track, though I gotta admit I loved Leslie. But nothing could beat watching the ponies run around the track on a nice day. Never cared much for those sloppy tracks when it rained." He hesitated, then whispered, "I think I'm ready to meet someone."

I was thinking it was a little late for that, but I understood. How would I feel if I didn't have Pam? So I played along, though didn't hold out much hope. "I'll help you. Finding a woman is right in my wheelhouse."

"Ever try those online dating sites?"

"Does a leopard have spots? So anyway, who are you living with?"

"My Aunt Irene, my mother's sister. She's my only living relative. She's 92. I'm running out of time. If I don't find someone soon my urn could end up in a garage sale or thrift shop. Someone will dump my ashes and use the urn for a candy dish or maybe even another body." Jerry's outline of a face crumpled with anxiety.

"I'm on it, Jerry. I'll get you hooked up, don't you worry."

That afternoon I sprawled out on the couch in our living room watching Dr. Oz, but something was gnawing at me beyond the doctor's pat and questionable tips for living longer. Jerry's forlorn, crumpled face kept coming to mind. I couldn't shake it. I clicked the remote off and flew over to the computer. Pam was at work so it was safe to go on. Never wanted my girl to see moving keys or changing screens.

I began with the online dating services to see if any had a section for the deceased. After all, I couldn't be the only dead person online. I surfed through Our Time, Zoosk, Tinder, eHarmony, JDate and ChristianMingle. Religion is meaningless after death, as is skin color and party affiliation. The living should learn from this. Judging from the profiles and photos, many of the applicants appeared to be dead. None, however, were. It seemed the only chance Jerry had of meeting a female spirit was to accidentally run into one. This was unlikely to happen in our building. We would have to expand our flying territory in Santa Monica considerably, something we may have been incapable of doing. At the very least we'd have to fly across Wilshire Boulevard. It was the best chance we had of snagging Jerry a good woman. Though actually any deceased but still flying woman would do.

A second option was to find another place for Jerry's urn so he'd be ready when Aunt Irene took her last breath. I began a new search. I Googled "urn placements" and came up with "Urn Match.com," "Urn Relocators International and Local" (their slogan: When your loved one needs a home away from your home), "Assisted Urn Support," "United Urn Lines," and "Country Urn Living." This last one was endorsed by Martha Stewart and, as you would expect, was tasteful but pricey. Still, how would we, as mere deceased beings, manage to communicate with any of these companies to get Jerry a pleasant resting place for his urn? It just wasn't going to happen.

I slumped over the keyboard in frustration. I didn't have the heart to tell him the chance of succeeding at either of these approaches was slim to none.

While I was in the midst of getting walloped by competing worries, it occurred to me that there was a terrific niche opening for an online dating business for the dead. Why hadn't anyone thought of this before? I could make a bundle. What would I call it? "Love in the Time of Coma," "A Match Made in Heaven," "Spirit Mates," "Rematch After You're Gone," "Stiff But Still Got the Stuff," "Death Mates.com." So many possibilities. But I didn't need money, which – while liberating – left me little motivation to start a business. Writing and submitting short stories online that I never got paid for was enough to keep my remaining brain cells active. I returned to worrying about Jerry, and decided we'd just have to try to find a female floater. Crossing Wilshire Boulevard would open us up to crowds of people. Hopefully there would be some dead among the living.

The next day Jerry and I waited in the lobby for someone to come and open the heavy glass front door. Larry walked by wearing shorts, a tank top and expensive Nike running shoes. A bright blue sweatband circled his balding head. Not a good look.

"Would you get a load of him?" Jerry said.

"I did all that shit myself before I kicked. Worked out at the gym, ran, rode a bike."

"How old were you when you hit the skids?"

"Just a couple of months from hitting sixty. What about you?"

"Sixty-two. Bad ticker." Jerry patted the scaly spot where his heart once was.

"Yeah, I'm pretty sure that's what got me too. Let's go," and with a whoosh, we passed Larry by and flew onto 4th Street. The sudden, rogue wind we set in motion in our wake caused Larry to look around apprehensively, but after a short pause, he adjusted his headband and took off in the opposite direction toward Montana Avenue.

Jerry and I made it almost to the corner of 4th Street and Wilshire. Our flying skills had been improving with daily practice, but neither of us had ever flown this far. Winded, we collapsed onto the curb to rest. "You OK?" I finally asked.

"Barely," he replied.

A Big Blue Bus came to a stop in front of us. A balding, wrinkled man who looked like he would be about our age if we were living heaved his bike with tremendous effort onto the rack in front of the bus. He appeared to be in the same sorry shape we were in, as he limped onto the bus.

"You thinking what I'm thinking?" Jerry asked.

"Hurry," and we rushed onto the bus, taking the seats reserved for the handicapped just before the door closed behind us. "Hey, Jerry, be ready to get off the next stop the door opens or we could be riding this bus a long time."

"Gotcha."

The bus stopped two blocks away and we quickly flew out. We were on the corner of 4th and Arizona, people surging around us. It was a busy area with stores, restaurants, apartments and office buildings.

"I know exactly where to go," I said, leading him in flight across the street to T.J.

Maxx. "This place is packed with women. We just need to find a dead one."

We entered the store, following closely behind two women carrying empty shopping bags. "Follow me," I said, and flew over to the pocketbooks; I sat on a bright pink suitcase in front of a large window facing a row of pocketbooks. "If we stay long enough, someone is bound to fly by."

"Hope so," Jerry said, coming to a landing on the blue carry-on next to me.

Time passed. We saw plenty of shoppers, but so far everyone was alive.

"Maybe we should start getting back." Jerry looked worried.

"We can always catch the bus. Relax."

And then it happened. A sparkling figure of a spirit flew around the corner and alighted beside a beige Calvin Klein. She was so focused on the bag she didn't see us.

I elbowed Jerry excitedly. "Hey, look. Over there."

Jerry had been gazing wistfully out the window at a La Salsa taco place. He turned around to check out what hopefully could be his mate. "She's a beauty, but I think she's out of my league," he said sadly.

"Confidence, my man, confidence. That's what the chicks gravitate to. Show no fear."

"Easy for you to say."

"Come on, let's go meet her," and I took him by the arm and pulled him over to her.

A short, stout white-haired woman rushed over to the Calvin and without hesitation, snatched it up. A hand belonging to someone else appeared on the beige handle. It was attached to a drop-dead blonde with fire in her eyes. Both these women were very much alive.

"It's mine, I saw it first," the blonde said. "You almost knocked me down pushing ahead of me like that."

"Mine," the older woman insisted. "The handbag is mine." She spoke with a thick accent, probably Russian.

"That's not how things are done in *this* country," said the blonde tugging on the handle.

"Mine," the older woman repeated, hanging tight. "Mine!"

A male employee stepped into the fray to mediate. Our female flier hovered above them, watching with interest. Jerry and I hovered behind her. After a few minutes they all walked off, the employee holding the bag. At this break in the action, I tapped the spirit on her shoulder. She turned to me with a start.

"Oh," she said. "You startled me."

"Sorry, "

"Did you see what happened? I loved that purse."

I couldn't empathize with her loss, having no frame of reference for being beaten out of a purchase of any kind. I found myself uncharacteristically at a loss for words, and realized I was way off my game. Had it been that long since I spoke to a good-looking woman? I struggled for something to say, anything at all. Not surprisingly, Jerry's also mute. "Come here often?" I finally asked. Oh, Jesus, did I really just say that tired old line?

"Yes," she answered smiling. "I live around the corner and love to shop, though now I have to do it vicariously."

"Nice handbag," Jerry said, joining the conversation smiling that great smile of his. The guy was a natural. If only he'd known this when he was alive.

"Yes," she said, "but there'll be more. They get shipments every day. That's what makes coming here so exciting."

"What's your name?" Jerry asked, taking over the conversation. Man was I out of practice. He didn't need my help at all.

"Caroline."

"A pleasure to meet you," Jerry said, leaning towards her and taking the outline of her hand in his.

Sparks flew. They had an instant connection. I swear I could actually see their scales flash.

Jerry was so enthralled with Caroline that he made the trip solo to the store three, maybe four times a week. In the beginning they split their time together between T.J.'s and La Salsa. Jerry told me he could taste the fish tacos as the two hovered over people eating at the outside tables. But after the first rush of love, Caroline lost all interest in La Salsa. "There's no point to it," she told Jerry. "It's not like we can eat."

"True, but I can say the same about your shopping."

"But I love to shop," she said.

"I love to eat," he said. And they proceeded to have the first of many arguments. If only things could remain as glorious as they appear to be when two people initially meet there would be no divorce or alimony, settlements, divorce lawyers, sunken finances, restraining orders, custody battles. I could go on.

One day, Jerry and I were sitting on a grassy area by the pool. The guy who's a ringer for Dr. Mancini was barbecuing burgers on the community grill. Jerry stared at them hungrily.

"Man, would I love to sink into one of those babies. Especially with bacon and cheese."

"I never get hungry anymore. Well, almost never. When I was alive I ate anything I could get my hands on after I smoked."

Jerry looked pensive. I thought he was imagining what those burgers tasted like, but it turned out he had something else on his mind: "All Caroline wants to do is shop. First it's bags, then shoes, then clothes. One day she spent our whole time together flying around housewares. Pots, pillows, sheets, dishes. Looking at that stuff is as bad as watching paint dry. Henry, she's driving me nuts. And talk about equal time. She refuses to go into that new sports bar I told you about, and it's right near T.J.'s. We went by the other day and they were running the afternoon races from Santa Anita on a big screen. I thought I died and ended up in heaven. I watched through the window while she whined and moaned about getting to the store. She gave me a headache, and I haven't had one since I croaked. I told her to go, that I'd meet her there. Truth is, we have nothing in common. Zilch."

I nodded to commiserate. Jerry continued. "Yesterday she flew over to the Banana Republic after T.J.'s. We'd already said our good-byes, but I decided to follow her. Curiosity, you know, thought maybe I'd catch her meeting up with another guy. I didn't think it could be possible that all the woman thinks about is shopping. So I'm flying behind her trying to keep up. Banana Republic's a long way from T.J.'s, you know. She almost killed herself getting there. Landed in a heap yards from the entrance. I keeled over myself. Way too long a flight, especially for nonstop. Anyway, she was so exhausted she didn't notice me laid out on the sidewalk. I'm on the ground like a deceased vagrant thinking she'll have the sense to rest a while, get up and fly home, right? But not her. The next shopper that comes along opens the door and Caroline follows her in. I should have known; there was a Sale sign in the window. I've had it."

"There's plenty more fish in the sea, Jerry," I said, though I had my doubts.

"When do you think Larry and Greg will get here?"

* * *

So that's how Jerry came to give up on love again, at least of the heterospiritual kind. We'd go to the sports bar a couple of times a week. Sometimes we watched the races, sometimes baseball or football. Whatever was on. Afterwards we'd take a short fly over to La Salsa for some taco browsing. We never went into T.J. Maxx. By the time we'd get the bus back to our building, Larry and Greg were usually home from work and smoking up a storm at the pool. If not them, there was bound to be someone else toking. Yeah, if the truth be told Jerry had become a stoner, but did it really matter at this stage? Nope, I assure you it didn't. What was important was that we were buddies. It was great to have a friend again; hadn't had one since I shoved off unless you count Pam. But she was alive, lots of limitations there.

And there was other good news. Aunt Irene was still going strong. Jerry and me, man, we had nothing to worry about. Nothing at all.

Chapter 4
LOVE IN THE TIME OF DEATH

One afternoon Jerry and I were hanging out at the pool. Santa Ana winds were blowing and the sky was an impossibly clear blue. We were sitting on top of a plastic patio table between Larry and Greg, catching their secondhand smoke.

"You psyched about tomorrow?" Greg asked.

"Major league chick city," Larry said.

Larry and Greg never stopped trying to score with the beautiful young women who inhabited many of the apartments in our building. That they met with little success didn't appear to alter their aspirations, but apparently they were seeking a fresh venue.

"Cabo San Lucas here we come," Greg said, passing the joint back to Larry.

"You hear that, Henry?" Jerry asked.

"Yeah. Larry and Greg are going to Cabo. Want to join them?"

"Never been to Mexico, but I'm not so sure. We don't know how they're getting there or how long they'll be gone." Worry crumpled Jerry's face.

"What difference does that make? We need an adventure. Are you in or what?"

Jerry breathed in some smoke-filled air. "But what if something happens to Irene while we're gone?"

"What are you worried about? Sure it's a bummer if Aunt Irene kicks, but what could you do if you were there when it happened? Nothing, right?"

"I guess." He hesitated, took another hit. "Alright. What the hell."

The next morning Jerry and I sat in wait in front of Larry and Greg's apartment, the two of us looking like something you might see on a bad LSD trip. We were used to our new exteriors by then, which actually resembled our old ones. But trust me, I freaked the first time I saw a fellow spook. So anyway, we were sitting around, talking about this and that, when their door opened. Quickly we got up and walked behind them as they wheeled their suitcases down the stairs and into the garage. After they loaded their luggage in Larry's trunk, we hurried into the car and sat on the back seat.

"We're off" Larry said, starting the car.

"Cabo, Cabo, Cabo," Greg said, smiling so wide I thought his face might break.

I looked out the window as we pulled out of the garage and into the alley. Another beautiful sunny day.

"This is so cool," I said.

"I really could use a couple of Xanax. I mean we don't know where we're going, Henry."

The dead, as you probably already surmised, are incapable of ingesting Xanax or anything solid or liquid for that matter. Luckily we could still inhale vapors. "What are you worried about? They'll light up a joint any minute."

They did, and soon enough Jerry was contentedly gazing out the window. We seemed to be headed to the airport, which could pose some logistical problems for us. Wouldn't want to take any chances with all those x-ray machines. But I figured if that's where we ended up we could just take a bus right back home. I breathed in some smoke to quell my own fears.

We drove past the airport and continued on the 405 until we got to San Pedro. Larry exited and followed the signs leading to the port. A cruise! These guys weren't such idiots after all.

"Jerry, man, we're going on a cruise. I love cruises."

"Always meant to take one, never did. Wanted to take the ex, but she said it wasn't for her. I think what she was really saying was that I wasn't for her. Oh, what the hell. What's passed is passed."

"You got that right. Time to party."

After they parked the car, we followed closely behind them as they walked into the terminal. If we lost them who knows whose cabin we'd end up in. The lines to check in were long, but everyone looked really happy. I didn't spot any fellow deceased fliers, but it was a big ship. There were bound to be a few dead women on board. Jerry had given up the search for a female companion after breaking up with Caroline. It was a real shame because at first, I thought he had finally gotten over his wife leaving him for their pharmacist. But again he swore off women, substituting sports and inhaling food smells, particularly Mexican. But I was getting the feeling that his interest in finding a mate might be rekindling. Cruise ships can do that to even the most romantically disillusioned. This probably harks back to that old TV show, *The Love Boat*, which I never watched. I swear it.

We got to the cabin and I was relieved to see it had a balcony. Always good to have a balcony, it being a second way to get in and out. The room had two single beds separated by a nightstand, and a desk, chair and sofa near sliders that led outside to a small balcony.

"Got to love this," I said, stretching out on the couch. "This is the life."

"Let's check out the buffet and the female cruisers," Greg said excitedly, dropping his carry-on on the carpeted floor. And before we had a chance to fly after them, they were gone, the cabin door clicking shut behind them.

"There are worse places to be stuck in," Jerry said, looking out at the ocean. "The slider's open. Let's go outside." The afternoon was bright and sunny. We were still docked, as the ship wouldn't leave until later in the day.

We stood outside, our scales quivering in the soft breeze. "Hey, Jerry, we can get to the balcony on either side of us without flying over the water. Let's see what's going on next door."

We flew over the divider, then peered through the glass into the cabin on our left. "Wow, look at this place. It has a bedroom, a living room, and two TVs. A suite! I've never seen one of these before. These people must have mega bucks."

"Yeah, the one-percenters," Jerry said, as he sat down on a chair on the spacious balcony and nibbled the outline of his finger.

Just then, a man and woman came into the cabin. They were laughing like they didn't have a care in the world. Somehow their laughter was different than how the rest of us ninety-nine percenters laugh. A platter of cheese and crackers and a bottle of champagne in a bucket of ice waited for them on the cocktail table near their open slider. In Larry and Greg's room there was a bottle of water with a $3.00 price tag around its neck. Jerry and I had front row seats to the rich and maybe famous. The man poured two glasses almost to the top and handed one to the woman. She was younger than him, and pretty good-looking. I figured him for 60, but the type who took real good care of himself. Her too. Well dressed, good shoes, expensive haircuts.

"I told you we'd do this one day," the man said.

"I never really believed it would happen, Richard."

"You know I would have left her if she hadn't..." Richard looked down at his carry-on. "You believe me, don't you?"

The woman didn't answer, saying a mouthful.

Richard raised his glass. "A toast to us. To our long and happy life together."

"Just one thing," she said.

"Anything for you, baby girl."

"Can you keep her outside? She's creeping me out."

"Not a problem." He bent over, unzipped the bag, and pulled out a sleek silver urn. A dead female right next door. Awesome.

"We hit pay dirt," I said to Jerry, as Richard carried the urn onto the balcony.

"She always loved the ocean," Richard mumbled, resting the urn on top of the wooden railing, as he stood staring down at the water. A menacing expression came over his face; his eyes looked cruel. Jerry and I went on high alert. Could Richard be thinking about dumping his wife before the ship even left shore?

He turned back round, slammed the urn onto an outdoor dining table, and hurried inside, closing the slider and drapes tightly behind him.

"Jesus, man. No love lost there," I said.

"Must have been cheating on her for years," Jerry lamented.

"Yeah, I know the type." Though I was no boy scout, I still felt badly for the poor woman, whoever she was.

"You know, Henry, she could be one of the dead dead."

"Let's hope not," I said, though experience had taught us that not all of the departed are able to function after demise.

"Let's try to rouse her," Jerry said, flying close to the urn.

"I don't know if that's such a good idea. Maybe she should come to on her own. Or not, as the case may be." I didn't want him to get his hopes too high.

"Come on. She'll respond or she won't. It's as simple as that. No harm in trying though." Jerry was back in the game whole hog.

"You're right. Go do your thing."

Jerry hovered over the urn just an inch or two away. "Hello in there," he shouted.

No response.

"She's probably a deadhead," I said.

"I'm not giving up so fast. Hello, hello. Are you in there?" he screamed, then tapped on the urn with one pointed, outlined finger.

I considered flying to the cabin on the other side of ours, when I heard a woman's voice emanate from inside the urn: "Richard, is that you?"

We were startled. Much as we wanted this chick to have some life left in her, we didn't expect she would.

"Richard?" a woman's sweet voice repeated.

I knew we had to help this broad out. This could be her first encounter with anyone since she died. But how do we let her down easy about what's happened to her?

"Richard's not here, but he'll be back soon," I said, thinking the next time she's in contact with Richard he may well be flinging her into the ocean.

"Who are you? Where am I? It's so dark, I may as well be dead."

Uh-oh, the D word. I looked over at Jerry, but he was at a loss for words. The ball was in my court. "Don't worry. It's all good. You're with friends now."

"Leslie and Ben are here?" she asked. "Have I been sick? Why is it so dark? Have I gone blind?"

"Sorry, Leslie and Ben aren't here. My name's Henry and my buddy here is Jerry. There's nothing to worry about. We're with you."

"I think I may remember something," she said.

"What's that?" Jerry asked.

"Yes, I remember now. I collapsed in my kitchen. I'd been reading a Gabriel García Márquez novel. All of a sudden there was terrible pain in my chest and back. The force of it was unbearable and I fell onto the tiled floor. Then my head hurt; I must have hit it when I fell. Through the window I could see it was getting dark. Thank goodness Marinelli was still there. She usually leaves by four, but she'd been catching up on some housework. I couldn't speak; the pain was overwhelming. She called for an ambulance, then tried getting Richard on the phone. He's my husband. But he didn't pick up. I remember riding in an ambulance. The sirens were so loud and we were going really fast. But I don't remember the hospital at all. Am I dead? Please tell me. I have to know."

Jerry and I hovered over her urn. "Please," she said, "you can tell me."

"Sorry to say, but yes, you have passed." Such a lame expression, one I try not to use. In cases like this, though, nothing else seemed appropriate.

"Passed," she repeated breathlessly. "Where am I then?"

"You're inside an urn. On a cruise ship. On the balcony. Jerry and I are dead, too. We're staying in the cabin next door."

"Where the hell is Richard?"

"Well...."

"He's with that woman, right?" We didn't answer. She was gaining velocity. "He's here with her. With Heather. Have you seen Heather? Blonde, tall, big fake breasts, bad cheek implants. He's been having an affair with her a couple of years. Before that there was Joan, and before her Carrie. Or maybe it was the other way around. So many years, so many women, who can remember? Especially at my age."

"Sorry to hear that," I said.

"Yeah," Jerry said. "I'm sure you are a lovely woman and didn't deserve..."

"My fault," she interrupted. "I should have left him years ago. I fell for his apologies, his empty promises to change, for the idea of love and family, and for the supposed good life. I missed my chance to find someone who truly cared about me. Too late to leave him now. Richard must be dancing on my grave, though as it turns out, he didn't buy me one. How the hell do I get out of this damn urn? I get depressed when I don't get enough light. I have seasonal affective disorder."

"I've got the same thing," Jerry said. "Don't worry, you'll get out. It could take some time, but it'll happen. And Henry and I will keep coming to check on you. What's your name?"

"Jennifer. Promise you'll come back soon?"

"Count on it," Jerry said, and we flew back to our cabin.

I was on my back resting on the couch after this taxing encounter. Jerry took over one of the twin beds. Larry and Greg hadn't returned.

"I hate to bring you down, Jerry, but if Jennifer can't break free of her urn before her husband throws her overboard, there's a chance she may not be able to partake in an afterlife. This could be the end for her."

"I was worried about that."

"Happened to a guy I heard about when I was at the crematorium. He didn't have time to develop afterlife skills before they threw him off the Venice Pier, urn and all, although in his case it was a See's candy tin. They say you need time to get out of your urn, learn to fly, figure out how to get around before your ashes get dumped. Unless, of course, you get to do some of the work before they cremate you. That's what happened to me. My ex Maxine took her sweet time deciding where I'd end up, so I stayed in the morgue longer than most. That's where I learned the ropes. But apparently Richard didn't waste any time torching Jennifer."

"My God, Henry."

"Best case scenario, he'll forget about dumping her for awhile."

Jerry's face rumpled with despair. "I'll help her. Keep her talking. I won't let her fade away. Forget the buffet. Go without me."

"No way. We're in this together, man." And so our vigil began.

A couple of days passed, and Jennifer still couldn't escape from her urn. Whenever Larry and Greg left the slider open, we'd fly over. Now that we were on open seas, wind and sea spray whipped our silvery scales, making the short trip to her balcony challenging, but Jerry was determined to be there for her.

"Don't worry, Jennifer," he said, on one of our jaunts to bolster her spirit spirits. "You'll be out in no time." But we both didn't really believe it.

"I'm getting antsy," Jennifer said. "This blackness is killing me."

We avoided saying the obvious. It was getting harder and harder for Jerry to leave Jennifer, but I convinced him to fly back to our cabin before Larry or Greg closed the slider.

That night Jerry and I were asleep on the sofa, his head on one end, mine at the other, when I heard tapping on the glass. At first I ignored it, exhausted from the gusty winds that afternoon. But I heard it again. Tap, tap, tap. Then more urgently. TAP, TAP, TAP! Larry and Greg were out cold after getting hammered at the disco on deck 16.

"Hey, Jerry, you hear that?"

"Now I do," he said, waking up. "Let's go look."

We flew to the slider. What we assumed must be Jennifer shimmered on the moonlit balcony on the other side of the glass. Even though much of her was covered with scales, you could tell she was a looker.

"It's Jen!" I'd never seen Jerry so excited.

She saw us, but we couldn't hear what she was saying through the door. We motioned to show her how happy we were that she got out of her urn. She motioned back smiling but looked tired. I always sucked at charades, and apparently Jerry did too. We made dismal attempts to tell her to fly back to her urn and stay there until the next day when we'd dock at Cabo. Looking confused and forlorn, she flew back over the divider.

"I'm worried," Jerry said, as we lay down on the couch.

"I wouldn't expect otherwise. Get some sleep. They'll open the slider when they get up."

"I can't stand to think of her alone outside like that." He tossed and turned the whole night. My friend Jerry was in love.

* * *

The three of us became inseparable, and Jerry and Jennifer were in love. The ship was great. We didn't run into any other deceased fliers but had a terrific time anyway. We enjoyed watching some especially large live cruisers at the buffet, which was open almost 24/7 on this cruise line. We had never imagined how much one person could eat. After finishing a jumbo-sized blue and white plastic platter filled with food, they'd leave it on the table and fill up another. You'd think they'd stop at two, but the biggest cruisers could put away three even four platters at one meal. And with the variety they brought to the table, we had more foods to smell. "I swear I'm hungry," Jerry would say. But that's impossible for the dead, even after partaking in a marijuana marathon with Larry and Greg. Yes, the imbeciles had thrown caution to the wind and brought pot on board, even though there was no smoking of anything allowed in the cabins or almost anywhere else. So far they hadn't been caught. Turned out Jennifer enjoyed a hit now and then. She told us she had been a hippie chick in the sixties, until she met Richard at Boston University. Funny, or not so much, the turns life takes you on.

I gave up my spot on the sofa so she could sleep over. No funny business though. Spooks are not capable of that kind of thing. But love, now that's a whole other story. The need for love doesn't dissipate with death.

One afternoon we were hanging out on Jennifer's balcony. The ship was docked in San Diego, its last stop before returning to Los Angeles. We hadn't seen Richard the entire trip except for the night at the pool party when he made a fool of himself attempting to line dance. Now suddenly the slider door jerked open, scaring the hell out of us.

"Oh, lord, it's Richard," Jennifer whispered.

"No worries. He can't do anything to you now," I told her.

Jerry took hold of her hand. Richard grabbed the urn. His face was sweaty and mean. Heather stood in the doorway, hands on her hips. Jen was right about the cheek implants. They looked especially ridiculous in the bright afternoon sun. I figured she had a good shot at malpractice.

"It's time, Richard," Heather said, devoid of emotion.

Now I've got to ask, what lunatic came up with the screwed-up notion that dead people should be hurled into the ocean, or a lake, stream, or pond for that matter? Jesus, man, we're not fish and never were. I couldn't think of anything more horrifying than having my remains floating in cold water. Even warm wouldn't work. You can keep Hawaii if that's the only way I was getting back there.

The three of us sat at the table, tense and waiting for the toss. Without saying a word, a prayer, or even good-bye, Richard strode to the railing, opened the top of the urn, and shook the ashes out into the sea below.

Jerry gasped, Jennifer looked stricken, I felt sick.

"You're safe," Jerry assured Jennifer.

"I know." Her pretty outline of a face smiled at him. Sure it took them more than a lifetime, but in the end they found one another.

"Fini," Richard said, slamming the lid on the urn, and brushing off the residue of ashes with thick, uncaring fingers. "Should I save this?"

"What for?"

"Yeah, you're right." And without turning around, he hurled the urn over his shoulder. It landed with an insignificant splash, then disappeared into the water.

"Let's go to the bar," Richard said. "Party time."

* * *

We got back home to Santa Monica and all was well. I was happy to be with Pam again, happy for the comfort and safety of my urn on top of her dresser. Jerry and Jennifer were downstairs with Aunt Irene. Our scales vaporize and disappear upon entering a vessel, so they were able to fit into Jerry's urn, snug as a bug in a rug, as they say. Death is good when you've got love and friends. Guess in that way it's no different than life. Hey, this could make a good episode of *The Love Boat*, if they ever bring the show back. Or maybe it could be the first episode of a new miniseries. Always wanted to write one of those. I knew just what I'd call it: *Love in the Time of Death*.

Chapter 5
THE EX FLIES

I was getting a nice contact high sitting next to Larry at a table overlooking the pool. He and his roommate Greg were far and away the biggest stoners in our apartment building. If I were still alive I'd have given them a good run for that distinction. The two of them always had the best marijuana, and when they weren't at work, they were usually at the pool, which was packed that late sultry summer afternoon. Looked like a Friday to me. Everyone was drinking, smoking and who knows what else. Chemically manufactured though it may be, they all seemed very happy. That is, except for my ex. Maxine. I watched as she stood glaring down at her neighbors from her second-floor balcony. She drank from a large water glass that wasn't filled with water. Maxine had always been into red wine, claimed it was the healthy alcohol choice. When we were married and I still had money she drank the expensive stuff, as if drinking Chateau Montrose 2005 instead of two buck chuck made her any less of a wino. These days she dragged home lower shelf half-gallon bottles of red from

CVS, whatever was on sale that week even if it came in a box. It irked her not to have money, but as things got tougher and tougher for me her alimony went down accordingly. Now, of course, she got nothing.

Maxine's face looked grim. I suspected she'd gotten too many left swipes on Tinder or a recent internet hookup had dumped her. No surprise there. At that very moment she was screeching at someone on her cell phone. I couldn't make out what she was saying and didn't feel like flying upstairs. I didn't care what went on with her, hadn't for years. In my semi-stoned state I was content to sit back and watch. There was still plenty of light to see that her face was red and the expression on it deranged. She had worked herself into one of her typical freak outs; she could never let anything go. She was no longer on the phone. Just drinking. Something must have really ticked her off, because she was slugging straight from the bottle. That woman could usually hold her liquor, but she was staggering around her terrace in a very un-Maxine-like way. She stopped to take a swig, then continued lurching, back and forth, back and forth. I assumed she'd pass out on her lounge chair before long. Eventually I lost interest and flew over to Jerry and Jennifer. They had just gotten to the pool. We were still the only spirits in the building unless some agoraphobic spooks were hiding out in somebody's apartment.

"Larry's got some great stuff, Jerry," I said smiling.

Jerry gave me the thumbs-up sign with one of his scaly fingers; Jennifer's face scales creased into a grin. "Catch you later, Henry," Jerry said, and the two took off in Larry's direction. And to think the guy didn't even known what a joint was before he met me.

I looked back up at Maxine's terrace. I fully expected to see her sprawled out on her lounge. Instead the top half of her body hung over the iron balcony railing; the bottle of red dangled from her hand. I watched it fall onto the grass below. I couldn't see her face, but I knew I'd never seen her this drunk. Healthy drink my ass. Red wine can be lethal. She'd have been better off smoking a few doobies. And then it happened. It was like watching a movie because I couldn't believe it was actually happening. Sure I'd often daydreamed about something befalling her, thought up countless ways my ex's demise could play out. But falling from a balcony? That was a bit grotesque even for my taste. But thar she blew. Head leading the way, she careened down, long hair flying in the breeze, silent as a bird in flight. Maybe she foolishly chased her fallen wine bottle, maybe she decided to voluntarily check out. In any case, she landed without fanfare on the grass; just a few feet over and she would have hit the concrete surrounding the pool.

I flew over. There was no blood. She laid on her side more peaceful than I'd ever seen her, though admittedly a bit disheveled. Maybe she was okay. A young woman rushed over. She kneeled and leaned in close to Maxine. "Are you alright?" she asked, softly patting my ex's arm.

Maxine's serene face was still. A man who looked like a handsome extra at a California pool party came by. "Is she passed out? I think she's the woman on the second floor near the trash chute. Never spoke to her. Can you tell if she's breathing?" he asked.

"Yes, I think so. I think she's breathing. She may have fallen from her balcony."

"No way! Are you okay, lady? Can you speak?" the Central Casting guy asked Maxine.

Silence.

"I'm calling 911," he said in a take-charge voice. He whipped out his iPhone as smoothly as John Wayne drew a gun.

I stood by taking this all in. She was breathing. She'd probably be fine. I never figured anything could actually kill her.

The ambulance arrived. Two large men lifted Maxine onto a stretcher and took her away. The party at the pool resumed. No one knew her except me and Pam.

The sky turned dark. More beer bottles opened, more weed was lit and passed around, pizzas from 800 Degrees were delivered. No one worried about the unhappy woman who lived on the second floor.

* * *

Many sunrises and sunsets passed near our building by the sea on 4th Street. I tried to catch as many of them as possible. Now that I no longer had eyes, though I could see quite well, I was able to look straight into the searing light without incurring injury or having to turn away.

So life and death continued on as before, although since I lived next door to Maxine I knew she had yet to return. A few times I discussed this with Jerry and Jen, but they had no answers. Then one day I heard Maxine's front door open and slam shut. I figured she was back, and flew onto her balcony, the scene of her unfortunate swan dive. I looked through the slider fully expecting to see my old nemesis. I was surprised when her cousin Eileen from New York walked into her bedroom. Maxine hated Eileen. Called her an opportunistic, phony, controlling, manipulating, devious witch, said her behind was even bigger than her mouth, and claimed, above all, that she was not to be trusted. Aside from the ass description, Maxine may well have been talking about herself. So there's Eileen, Maxine's closest living relation, scavenging through her belongings, the great majority of which were originally mine.

Eileen was talking into her cell phone, apparently making a list for the moving company of what to ship to New York and what to leave in the apartment. In her unmistakably Brooklyn accent she said: "Take chest of drawers, nightstands, desk, chair and floor lamp. Leave bed, headboard and ugly purple velvet upholstered chair. Wow, it's freaking hot in here." She opened the slider, giving me full access. I entered Maxine's apartment perturbed that this Machiavellian nightmare was taking possession of my beloved worldly goods. The question of what the hell happened to Maxine crossed my mind, but I was too intent on watching her cousin defile my belongings to dwell. I felt...violated.

I followed her into the living room. "Nothing much in the living room," she reported into her phone, wiping the sweat from her brow. "The cocktail table is a maybe." A maybe! What a moron. It was a vintage Knoll that had never been refinished, almost perfect condition and worth a small fortune. After I died and Maxine's shithead lawyer succeeded in ripping me off yet again, Maxine was given my apartment keys; I'd been living in a cheap Beverly Hills rent controlled one bedroom my last few years. From my mantel vantage point where Maxine kept my urn, I had watched as she and some guy carried the Knoll table into the Hollywood Hills house. They also lugged in several packing boxes filled with stuff she hadn't legally been able to grab from me in the first go-round. Almost killed me all over again. Not long after that, or so it seemed to me, the house in the hills ended up in foreclosure; that's Maxine's karma for you. Well, good then, Eileen was passing up one of the best pieces in the place.

I wondered what this imbecile would decide about the artwork. There was a signed Picasso pen and ink drawing hanging over an ugly end table that Maxine brought with her from a prior marriage. (She'd gone through two other suckers before me.) Eileen barely gave the Picasso a look, and it had to be worth five or six figures by then. I bought it years ago soon after selling *Herald Square*.

Eileen entered the kitchen. I followed her behind which was, as Maxine phrased it, double wide. It would be difficult to get past her in tight quarters. Regardless, she eventually found a mate. I only met the guy once. A dentist with a matching rear. "That's a cute picture," she said aloud, looking at a colorful framed print from an '80s Picasso Retrospective. She spoke into the phone: "No artwork except for the framed Picasso print in the dinette." Unless someone who knew something got here fast, my Picasso could end up in the alley dumpster. But at least Eileen wouldn't have it.

* * *

Pam was at work and I was stretched out on the yellow beach lounge on our balcony. I'd prefer something with padding, but no matter, I was feeling pretty mellow. I had just come from the pool. Larry was there smoking like a madman, nobody else around. I stuck close by him, got sufficiently twisted and flew back upstairs. I was snoozing, peaceful as all get out, when a familiar voice seared through what was left of me.

"Well, look who's here. I'll be damned, and I suppose I am. If it isn't Henry Davis. I'd say in the flesh, but clearly you don't have any." The laughter that followed was diabolic.

I was afraid to look. I thought if I didn't move maybe she'd go away. I was fully awake now and completely horrified. It was Maxine, no mistaking that god awful voice; it could crack an egg. She sat on the divider between our apartment balconies, arms straight down holding on, legs tightly crossed. I guess she wasn't taking any more chances. She resembled Maxine except, excuse the repetition, she had no skin, organs, hair or blood, and she was covered with transparent scales. So there was the answer to my question: my ex had bought the farm.

"Fuck, Henry, have you been here the whole time and I didn't know it?" She looked ready to blow.

I said nothing. Anything at this point could bring her to a full boil.

"Well, have you?"

"Yeah," is all I could manage. I hadn't felt this screwed up since before my demise. I hoped she wasn't planning to stick around long.

"Jesus, you've been spying on me for years. Watching me have sex, watching me take a shower, getting off to me undressing. Gross. I should have you arrested."

"Don't flatter yourself," I said, regaining some of my spunk.

"Admit it, you old piece of shit, you've always been sex-obsessed."

"Not when it comes to you," I shot back. This was getting ugly, too ugly for such a mellow day. "Get off it, Maxine. Since you threw my urn at Pam, I haven't been inside your apartment."

"You didn't have to be inside. You could see plenty lurking from the balcony."

"Nope. Never. Except for after your fall..."

"Go on," she said, her scales glistening with fury. I'd never seen that before, not on any of the spirits I'd encountered. I was wary, but at the same time fascinated. Illuminated by the sun, her fluttering scales exploded in a brilliant light show that was better than the old Joshua light shows at the Fillmore. I wished Jerry and Jen were here to see.

"Your cousin Eileen came by." I spoke slowly, watching her face for signs of a major freak out, getting ready to bail over the railing if need be.

"Oh, fuck! Is that why there's nothing left in my apartment? Fat ass took it all."

"Not exactly. She took some stuff, mostly from the bedroom. The moron didn't take the cocktail table or the Picasso."

"Where the hell are they?"

"A guy from Out of the Closet came and took what her movers left behind. Some of their customers hit the jackpot. Maybe they don't even know it yet."

"Couldn't you stop her? You know how much I hate that woman."

"Have you lost it completely? What could I do? Give me a break, Maxine. I'm dead."

"I suppose," she said, but didn't seem convinced.

"Can I ask you something?" I said.

"What?"

"Did you....deliberately...you know, jump?"

She turned away. I refrained from repeating the question. If the broad didn't want to tell me, why should I care?

She turned back around. "Are you nuts? What would I do that for? Life was good. I was seeing someone. Very seriously. A doctor. Head of something or other at UCLA. Radiology, yeah, he's head of radiology. Handsome son of a bitch. Has a house in Bel Air. You'd love it. Mid-century, a Richard Neutra. It was an accident. I had a little too much wine. I was due for my period and had taken a Valium. I never drink when I take Valium, but I forgot I'd taken it. It was an accident, Henry. Plain and simple."

So there it was. The tell, tells actually. She *always* drank when she took Valium, and there was no rich, handsome, doctor boyfriend. Maxine committed suicide, no doubt about it. Saving face. She may be dead but she still had her pride. So why rub it in? "Yeah, of course. That's what I thought."

We both got really quiet. My high was ancient history. Shocking as it might be, I felt sorry for her. She was so forlorn, so alone.

She looked down at the cracked cement floor that desperately needed a coat of paint. "I don't have anywhere to go, Henry. I won't stay long. I promise. I'll figure something out."

Fuck me, I thought, but said, "No worries. Stay as long as you need to."

We could have fit, but I refused to let Maxine sleep inside my urn. The maniacal woman actually suggested this. When I nixed the idea straight away she said, "You sure you don't want to sleep with me, Henry? C'mon, it'll be like old times." The scales surrounding her eyes fluttered.

"You may not be expired long enough to know this, but the dead are incapable of having sex, Maxine."

"Well, no, I didn't know that. I mean, how would I?" She looked at me coyly. "We can still snuggle, honey bear," she said, using the name she used to call me way back when.

If I'd eaten, I would have chucked my lunch. This chick was certifiable. Still, I wasn't ready to tell her how I really felt, but no way would she stay in the bedroom I shared with Pam. I had to put her as far away as possible; I relegated her to a piece of Mexican pottery, a good-sized bowl, on the kitchen counter.

Time passed. I tried to avoid running into her, but she was always floating around, especially when Pam was at work. It drove me nuts, but so far she was on her best behavior. It reminded me of her act before we got hitched. Thoughtful, selfless, patient, kind, free of neurosis or psychosis for that matter, a real sweetheart; as I would later discover, she put on one hell of a show, giving no hint what lay beyond that carefully constructed façade. Needless to say, I had no clue who I married.

Some things remained constant. Just like when she was alive, my ex never went to the pool and never partook of weed. She didn't know we could still get high from secondhand pot smoke. She never was a stoner, said marijuana made her eat whereas wine just made her pass out. Different strokes, as they say. And even though she was clearly in a depressed state, I didn't tell her there was a cure within easy flying distance now that Valium and wine were no longer an option. The last thing I needed was to have her hanging out at the pool. The woman had an addictive personality. She would stalk Larry and Greg and anyone else holding 24/7. So far she hadn't clocked me, although she often asked how I got to be so calm now that I'm dead. My answer to her was that death hits some people that way. "Lucky," she said, then drifted into another room to lick her wounds. I was almost certain she wasn't looking for a place to move to. I had yet to see her leave the apartment; she even stayed off the balcony, although that was understandable. To my dismay, I believed Maxine had become agoraphobic. I knew somehow I must expand her horizons, take her on some flights around the neighborhood, starting short and easy, then branching out. It was the only chance I had to get rid of her.

* * *

It wasn't easy getting Maxine to leave the apartment. She resisted my many friendly invitations to go flying, even on days when the weather was perfect and a short trip to Palisades Park overlooking the ocean might be doable.

"Let's stay home and watch TV," she said, settling onto Pam's sofa in front of the tube. She worked the remote with the skill of the living, her scaly fingers navigating her program search.

"Don't you get sick of television? It's all you do," I said, as I sat on a chair on the far side of the room. I didn't get too close. She'd already made a few lunges at me in an attempt to be romantic.

"You do hog the computer, honey bear," she said sweetly.

Who was this pleasant person? Yes, I was guilty of computer hogging, but in my defense I needed to get my writing time in when Pam wasn't home. You wouldn't be reading this if I didn't. But the real Maxine would sulk and scream about this inequity, then viciously demand equal screen time and copious apologies. Instead, this one smiled seductively and said, "Come, sit next to me. Remember when we used to love watching old movies together? You always made the popcorn."

Clearly she had become delusional. I had to get her flying or she'd stay here forever. And that may be a very long time. "I'm going out," I said cheerfully. "It's a beautiful day. Come with me. We'll have a great time. Like the old days," and I smiled my best Henry "the player" smile. I knew I was beginning to give her false hope, but I was officially desperate.

"You look so handsome when you smile, Henry. You should smile more often."

"Let's go," I said, as I took her hand and pulled her off the couch.

"We haven't held hands in so many years," she said, the scales on her cheeks blushing a pale pink.

Okay, okay, I was a cad leading this poor, dead, depressed woman on. But what other recourse did I have?

Our first fly took us around the corner to 3rd Street. The next day we switched directions and reached the north side of Wilshire Boulevard. My hope was that in this crowded area we'd meet up with a deceased flyer, possibly someone Maxine could hook up with, male or female; at that point it didn't matter which. A roommate, I had to find her a roommate.

After several trips, I decided my best bet was to get her to T.J. Maxx. I'd run into the departed there before. The store was a magnet for dead shoppers who kept their addictions going vicariously. Chicks mostly. Hopefully one would be happy to take on a new roommate.

The only problem was that Maxine was never a fan of T.J. Maxx or any other discount store. When we were married she had Bloomingdale's, Nordstrom and Neiman Marcus cards. I was hoping she'd lowered her expectations when she hit the financial skids, especially after the alimony stopped. Yeah, like any other serious shopper with money woes, she must have switched shopping destinations. I decided to feel her out.

"So what do you think about going shopping?" I casually asked, as we flew down the stairs and into the modest lobby leading outside. It had gotten easier to get her out of the apartment, I'll say that much.

"Have you forgotten we're dead, Henry?" she smiled, gliding to a stop by the large glass front door.

"Window shopping. Isn't that what they call it?" I fondled her arm to encourage her. Probably not the best idea.

"I guess. But where would we go? Bloomingdale's and Nordstrom are too far." She looked so wistful. Apparently she'd given up on Neiman's entirely, not realizing that we could take the Wilshire Boulevard bus there.

"I know," I said, as if just coming up with the idea. "T.J. Maxx is less than two blocks away."

Her scales flipped downward in sorrow. "Oh, that place. I had to shop there at the end. I had my old credit cards put in my maiden name but could hardly afford to buy anything. Not even when they had sales."

My disappointment at this turn of events was obvious. I'd never get her inside T.J.'s. I was silent as we followed behind a live young woman who opened the lobby door. "What a wonderful idea," she said, switching gears, scales returning to neutral. "I don't know if I can fly that far yet, but I'm willing to try."

I was so screwed. Like I said, this was not the Maxine I knew. My real ex would have shrieked, "You idiot, I won't ever step foot into a shit hole like that again. You truly have lost it, A-hole." I may be an idiot, but I knew she was intent on remaining in her Mexican bowl by channeling a nice person. I pushed this reality aside; I couldn't let any opportunity to pawn her off on someone else pass. "That's my girl. Let's give it a fly." I took her hand in mine and we floated slowly down 4th Street. We crossed Wilshire Boulevard, flew to the end of the block, then waited for a shopper to open the door. It didn't take long and we were in.

We had been flying around the store a while when I spotted him in the women's department. He was an older man, probably late seventies, sprightly flying over the racks and fingering the clothing. I figured he was transgender or a cross dresser in his day, perhaps a drag queen. This was of no importance to me. He had the one major component in a potential roommate I was looking for: he was dead. I approached him.

"Hey, how's it going?" I asked. Maxine was preoccupied in the jewelry department.

"Oh, a fellow spirit. How nice," he said.

"I'm Henry, Henry Davis. I live just up the street."

"Ben Cohen. I'm around the corner. One of the newer buildings, a lovely apartment." He continued touching the dresses.

"Been in L.A. long?" I asked, waiting for the right time to introduce him to Maxine.

"About twenty years. Moved here when I retired. I'm from New York. I was in the rag business. Dresses. Never lost my interest. Keeps me busy, especially since Alice passed."

My ear scales perked up. A dead man without a spouse! And apparently old Alice is a dead dead. "I have a good friend I'd like you to meet, Ben."

"Is she here?"

I pointed in Maxine's direction. "That's her over there. Pretty good-looking, wouldn't you agree?"

We flew in for a closer look. Maxine was perusing some fake diamonds. I wondered what happened to the real ones I gave her. Probably had to sell them to pay the rent. Well, it looked like her problems wouldn't be my problems for long. This guy was perfect for her.

"I don't think she's for me," he said, killing my reverie.

"Why not?" I asked, struggling to hide my alarm.

"Nice try, but no tomato." He winked.

"What do you mean?"

"She's your ex, right? You can't stand the sight of her, but you're trying to let her down easy, trying to find someone to take over for you. She's trouble. I wasn't born yesterday, you know. It's written all over her. A bona fide ball breaker excuse the expression. Nice meeting you, Henry. And better luck next time." Ben hurried back to the dresses.

Jesus, I was stuck with Maxine forever.

* * *

Disposing of Maxine became a full-time obsession. When I wasn't actively schlepping her around town, I was plotting our next excursion. I couldn't concentrate on my writing, no longer enjoyed getting stoned at the pool (well, maybe just a little), didn't even have enough stamina to enter into Pam's dreams. I was a dead man. Okay, we already knew that, but I'd lost my zeal. I focused on one thing only: expunging Maxine.

My OCD was in full bloom; I was in desperate need of my old meds.

Our trips to T.J. Maxx took on greater urgency, for me that is. So far Maxine went along for the ride wherever I suggested. Often it was T.J.s, but I threw in Palisades Park, a bench near Barnes and Noble or a trip to Joe's to smell the pizza just to keep her off track. I worried that at any moment the real Maxine would break through her amiable facade. I had to find her a roommate and fast.

One day we were flying around housewares; Maxine had developed a particular fondness for this section of the store. "OMG, look at this blanket, Henry," she said, as if I would actually care. "It's a Ralph Lauren. I must go see if they have the matching sheets and pillowcases." She whipped around the corner.

I was fucked. How long could I keep this up? I hated this store, had no interest in anything in it except for those who had bitten the dust, and we barely ran into any. There was one, an elderly French woman, but the language barrier was a real deal breaker. I tried to remember my high school French, but couldn't get past "Come on tally vu," (disregard the spelling).

I turned the corner looking for my ex. I was so astonished at what I saw that I sunk onto a stack of tablecloths. From this perspective I watched as Maxine and a woman spirit engaged in a spirited conversation about designer sheets. Initially I was too excited to move, but curiosity won out and I flew over to them. They were so busy talking they didn't notice me at first. Finally, a smiley-faced Maxine said, "Oh, Henry, this is Caroline."

I was blown away. Of all the spirits to run into, this was one I actually knew. Caroline turned and looked at me. "Oh, hi, Henry," she said. "Haven't seen you for a long time. How is Jerry doing?"

Oh kel bon chance, I thought, more French coming back to me. Caroline lived on 5th Street, right around the corner. As long as she hadn't moved in with Ben Cohen, I stood a chance of handing Maxine off to her.

"Caroline, so great to see you. You're looking good," I said. Caroline was very pretty, scales and all; Maxine looked envious.

"You two know each other?" Maxine asked with venom, her toxic self making a surge.

"Jerry's old girlfriend," I quickly said, patting Maxine's scaly shoulder. "We didn't know each other well at all, and I haven't seen her since they broke up." Maxine looked relieved, and her poison dissipated.

The two female spirits made plans to meet the next day, and Maxine and I took off for home. I was anxious to get to the pool to celebrate my good fortune. Things were definitely looking up.

Having few other outlets, Maxine's shopaholism came to the fore. She began flying off to T.J. Maxx and even Banana Republic and the Gap without me. She always met up with Caroline. They didn't stop to smell the lunches, just went directly to the racks. Maxine always came back exhilarated.

"You won't believe what we found today at Banana," she'd say excitedly. I feigned enthusiasm, and she'd babble on with detailed descriptions of what she and Caroline saw on their most recent trip. She was gone almost every day. I was free again to hang at the pool and get twisted. I was afraid of becoming overconfident, but I believed her days residing with me were numbered.

One late afternoon after returning from a shopping expedition, Maxine flew onto the terrace where I was resting. The expression on her face was solemn. Damn, she's had a blow-out with Caroline. I didn't dare say a word.

"I've got something to talk to you about, Henry."

I nodded for her to continue.

"I know we've been getting along great, better than ever really. You know how much I enjoy your company, and my bowl is truly lovely." I was gaining hope; I knew without a doubt that Maxine hated Mexican pottery. Mexican food too, which only proved the woman was a moron. Still, I remained silent.

"Don't be upset, honey bear, but I've decided to move in with Caroline. She's closer to the stores and we have so much to talk about. I know you got used to having me here, but it will be easier for me at her place. She took me to see her apartment today. It's in a much newer building. It has a beautiful lobby, AC and gorgeous wood floors. You know I always hated carpet, especially when it's old."

I was speechless. "Are you okay, Henry? I'll stay if you really, really want me to."

Time to jump in before the broad changed her mind: "Just a little surprised is all. It has been terrific having you here" (had I really just said that?!), "but I fully understand why it will be better for you at Caroline's."

"You're so understanding, Henry. And we'll still see each other. It's not like I'm moving to the Valley."

"Yeah, we can meet for lunch. When are you planning to go?" I ask, trying to curb my enthusiasm.

"Tomorrow, honey bear. I'm sure going to miss you." She flew over me and put what was left of her lips to the top of my head where my hair used to be. I worried she would stay there a while; I lay still as a corpse, praying she doesn't grope the space where my privates once were as a parting gift. Fortunately before long, she zipped back up. "I'm going to get to sleep early. Big day tomorrow. Night, Henry," and she headed into the kitchen.

* * *

She was gone! Flew out early the next morning. Before leaving, she'd tapped on my urn a couple of times. I pretended to be asleep. Didn't want to take any chance she'd change her mind. I waited for the coast to be clear, exited my urn and flew around the apartment, checking each room. The kitchen was my last stop, and the Mexican bowl was gloriously empty.

I needed to celebrate and flew down to the pool. Greg was smoking a doobie before he left for work. I leaned in close and breathed in the marijuana-laced air. He lit up a second. Did he know I was there rejoicing in my Maxine-less status? Nah, of course not, he's just a stoner, is all.

I slipped outside the building and gazed at the ocean shimmering in the distance. What a place! While basking in the California sun under the swaying palms an idea for a new short story came to me. With worry no longer consuming me, I was thinking clearly again. I flew back to Pam's apartment via the balcony, and hovered over the computer in her bedroom, my legs floating straight out behind me. Soon my fingers started to click the opening of the story on the keyboard. Peace had been restored in apartment 202. I was free.

Chapter 6
GOOD NIGHT, IRENE, GOOD NIGHT

Death was going pretty well. Nothing much to complain about now that Maxine had gone. At first I worried she'd come back. In fact, this became a recurrent nightmare of mine. I wouldn't fly anywhere near T.J. Maxx, and also steered clear of Banana Republic. Once when I was on the south end of the Third Street Promenade I thought I saw the two of them, Maxine and Caroline, scaly arm-in-arm, looking in the window of a shoe store. I made a fast retreat home via 4th Street. Maybe it was two other spirits, but I wasn't about to wait around to find out.

I decided to try to live (you know what I mean) in the moment. When I was alive I found this extremely challenging. I took a couple of yoga classes, hoping to find my center and all that shit, but it wasn't happening for me. I was too anxious, always worrying about the future or ruminating over the past. Except for when I imbibed. A pot and beer combo usually worked, sometimes with a little Ativan thrown in. I suppose if someone had to put me in a category "pothead" would do, but I never (okay, almost never) started smoking before four in the afternoon, and never partook while I was writing. Croaking cured me of most of my neuroses; it was nothing short of a miracle. But when Maxine came back from the living, that was a whole other story.

I took up the issue of ex-wife-induced post-traumatic stress with Jen and Jerry. Jerry wasn't one for introspection, but Jennifer used to be a shrink. We had some good talks and she turned me on to some interesting websites about conquering fear. So I was well on my way to better mental health, when Jerry's Aunt Irene collapsed in the laundry room. The wall fan wasn't working as usual, and it was a blazing hot afternoon. Lucky for Irene, Pam had just come in to throw her stuff in the dryer, and found Irene splayed out on the cement floor. Always so well-mannered even when down and out for the count (she came from another era), Irene said to Pam, "I'm terribly sorry to bother you, but if you can spare the time, would you please help me to my feet. I'm certain I'll be able to return to my apartment once I'm standing." The two women had never spoken before, which is often the case in apartment buildings these days. Years back everyone knew all their neighbors, which apartment they lived in, who they lived with, how rich or poor they were, and what they ate for dinner the night before. Now it's even money you don't know your next-door neighbors and they don't know you.

But it was clear to Pam that Irene was old, really old, and there was no way she was going to move her. Good thing Pam had her phone with her. She quickly called 911. At the time, I watched everything unfold as I sat atop a washing machine. Having just returned from the pool I was somewhat stoned, but quickly assessed the situation as dire. Dire for Irene first off; dire for Pam who always tried so hard to do the right thing; and dire for Jerry and Jen, who resided with Irene. What was to happen to them if she kicked? Where would their urn end up? Should they remain in Irene's apartment when new people moved in, and inhabit a substitute vessel? Or perhaps free spirit it with no vessel at all?

My anxiety surged directly to high. I wanted to race back to the pool to inhale more of Larry's secondhand smoke, but there was no way I could abandon Pam even though I was absolutely no help. If only I were alive!

Pam kneeled next to Irene. "Stay still for now and rest. I called for help. They'll be here soon. They'll know what to do."

"You must be an angel," Irene said. Did she think she was dead already?

Pam stroked Irene's arm and smiled reassuringly. She had the most beautiful smile, but I could tell she was upset. The ER people arrived, and just like with Maxine, they hauled Irene away on a stretcher. There was some blood on the floor where her head had been. I didn't know how to break the news to Jerry.

The next morning Jerry, Jen and I were sitting on a bench overlooking the ocean in Palisades Park. It was a warm, cloudless day, and when I gazed into the shimmering distance it seemed like nothing in this world could possibly be wrong. I attempted to stay in the moment, just for a moment, but then Jerry said, "Aunt Irene didn't come home last night."

Yeah, I should have told him as soon as it happened, I just didn't have the balls. When we had gotten back to our apartment after the ambulance took off, Pam was all shook up. From the window I saw Larry and Greg smoking at the pool with a couple of other neighbors and couldn't resist flying down from our balcony to join them. I stayed longer than I planned and by then I was pretty wasted. Didn't have the wherewithal to fly back upstairs, so I took the staircase, holding tight to the railing and taking my sweet time. I sat on the floor outside Pam's apartment and waited for her to open the door; finally she came out holding a bag of trash. I flew past her and rushed into my urn completely spent. Sue me, but I fell asleep. I dreamt about dirty cement floors, flying angels and Pam breaking up with me when we were in college because she found out I was screwing Susan Segal. By the time I got up, Pam had left for her office, the sun was shining and I had my work cut out for me. I decided the park was the best place to tell Jerry the sad truth about his aunt, so I talked him and Jen into flying there with me.

"Henry, did you hear what I said? Irene never came back to the apartment yesterday." Jerry's face was a crumpled mishmash of scales and he was all humped over, elbows on his knees; he appeared to have aged a hundred years in one day. Jen was solemn as she sat close by him.

"She collapsed in the laundry room. Yesterday afternoon. I should have told you right away. Pam found her. She called an ambulance. Irene was able to talk, but Pam told her not to move. They came pretty quick and took her to the hospital. I heard them say Saint John's. I'm so sorry, Jerry."

"I've got to get over there. Poor Aunt Irene. Do you think she'll be alright?"

"Sure, Jer. She looked fine. Really. I'll go with you."

"Me, too," Jen said. So we stood up and flew toward Santa Monica Boulevard to catch the bus up to 21st Street, passing the ocean view Ferris wheel on the pier, and people of all stripes who walk along Palisades Park. With only Aunt

Irene on our minds, we took the short bus ride to the hospital.

People constantly go in and out of Saint John's front doors, so we had no trouble getting in. Once inside the vast shiny lobby, the problem was how to find Aunt Irene.

"I spent my last few days here. I gotta tell you, there are worse places to be. Real nice for a hospital. And sunny; that's important when you're sick as a dog," Jerry said.

"Where should we start looking?" I asked, impressed by the pleasant surroundings. There had been a whole lot of darkness where I ended up.

"The cafeteria," Jerry said, and led us to a bank of elevators. "Some deceased fliers are usually hanging out there. Maybe Big Ed's still around. When I was in the morgue Len, a fellow flier, told me that a guy named Ed had been living in the cafeteria since 2004. Len claimed he saw him himself, that he was tall and strong with a full head of long blonde scales. It was unusual for any of us to have scales of any color. He described him as god-like, an urban legend of the hospital variety. Ed told Len that he grew up in New York City, then spent a couple of years in the South. He took up singing and guitar, acquired a southern accent and changed his name to Chance Lane. Came out to the coast to break into the music business, but never made it. After he gave up on a music career, he went back to being called Ed and worked as a carpenter. When he croaked he had no family to speak of, close friends were all gone, no place to go. The state cremated him, and he found his way back to Saint John's. Len said he loved to smell the turkey burgers. Apparently they were so good you couldn't get a seat in the cafeteria on Tuesdays."

"That's some weird shit," I said.

"Yeah, but would you have thought you'd be flying around Santa Monica like this before you shoved off?"

"Only when I was seriously twisted."

In the cafeteria Jerry stopped to peruse the offerings. No turkey burgers, so apparently it wasn't Tuesday. A dark brown stew of unknown origin floated in a large steel tray, and there was some spaghetti that looked like it came from a can. Not many takers around.

"Look! Over there! That must be Big Ed," Jerry said excitedly. He pointed to a large spirit fitting Ed's description sitting at a table with four spirits of differing ages and sexes.

We flew over. "Ed, you're still here," Jerry said, scales quivering with excitement.

"Where else would I be? Sorry, not sure I remember you."

"We never met, but your reputation was legend down in the morgue. I see you've got company."

"Yeah, we're like family. Dave's been here almost as long as I have. Gary and Alan came in together: car crash on the 10 after an Eagles concert. Our newbie is Alice. None of us had family at the end. Now we do." The scales surrounding his lips flipped into a big grin. His blonde scales were long and wild just like they'd been described. From a distance he looked like a rock 'n' roll star, sort of a mix between Robert Plant and Bon Jovi.

"I hear you loved those turkey burgers."

"They tweaked the recipe a couple of times, but they're still worth smelling."

"Meet my girlfriend Jennifer and my friend Henry. We live on 4th Street. Took the bus here to find my Aunt Irene. They brought her in by ambulance yesterday. Can you help us find her?"

"That's easy. They take all the ambulance riders to the ER. Let's go. See you guys later." Ed nodded to his friends and we took off.

We flew through the ER, checking out every gurney. Doctors and nurses walked softly and spoke in hushed tones; visitors looked worried. It was tense in the ER, not a place anyone would want to spend time. I didn't know much about it, but I supposed the hope was to be transferred to a bed upstairs, proof the doctors thought you had some life left in you. I worried about Aunt Irene. She didn't look good there on the laundry room floor, her face pale and withered. She could be dead already.

I was so anxious about flying into Irene's dead body that I lost track of where Jerry, Ed and Jen had gone until I heard Jerry scream: "There she is!"

I followed his voice to a white curtained area. Aunt Irene was flat on her back on a gurney covered to her neck with a white sheet, her long silver gray hair the only color in the tableau. She was hooked up to machines and wasn't moving. Jesus, I thought, no way could she come out of this.

Jerry sat by her side and put his scaly hand on hers. "I'm here, Aunt Irene. I'll stay as long as you need me to."

Irene's breathing was shallow. A nurse came in and checked the machines. A doctor followed shortly after. "Next of kin?" he asked.

"None so far. Still checking."

"I don't think she'll make it."

Jerry and Jen looked stricken. We stayed a long time. I counted at least four shift changes. The three of us huddled together on the floor. We must have fallen asleep, because we woke with a start when one of the machines began emitting a harrowing buzzing sound. At first no one came in to fix it. That noise could wake the dead. Except of course it didn't. It couldn't wake Irene. While we were sleeping, Aunt Irene had slipped through to the other side. The expression on her face was peaceful. A nurse entered the curtained cubicle and did something to the machine that stopped the noise. A doctor arrived in short order.

"She's gone," he announced, then scribbled on a clipboard. "You know what to do," he said to the nurse, and left.

"Maybe she'll come back to us," I said, though didn't hold out much hope.

Jerry cried without tears. "Do you think so?"

"I do, Jerry. I really do."

"She could be one of the dead dead, you know," he said.

"I think she'll make it. Give her time."

A short while later, we followed along as Irene's gurney was pushed down a long hallway and into an elevator. I knew where she was headed; I'd gone through this before in a different hospital. The elevator opened and the young male orderly pushed Irene down another hall and into a room with an unmarked black door. The morgue. It was cold as ice in there, and a few other bodies lay in wait around the room. Irene exhibited no sign of gaining re-entry. We stayed with her a long time. More bodies arrived, others departed. Irene's gurney remained in the corner. She wasn't coming to.

"I think she's really gone," Jerry said sadly.

"Give it more time. Remember what happened with Jen?"

"That's true."

So we waited. And waited. And waited. By that time our scales were frost-bitten or at least felt like they were. "We should go home and come back tomorrow," I said.

"I don't know."

"We could all use some rest, Jerry."

Finally he agreed. When we got to our building I worried that Jerry and Jen wouldn't be able to get back inside Irene's apartment, but the balcony slider was open just as Irene left it before her departure. I fell asleep on Irene's living room couch next to the French Provincial end table that held Jerry and Jennifer's urn.

The next day we were back at Saint John's. We waited by the door to the morgue until an orderly came along with a fresh body. We hurried in behind them. Anxious to get to Irene, we rushed past the new guy when we heard him say, "Hey, where the fuck am I? Is this some kind of a joke? Where's Mike and Johnny? And what the hell happened to my Budweiser? It was almost full."

Now this was impressive. Apparently this guy came to almost as soon as he passed. None of us had ever seen that fast a rebound although mine, I must admit, was almost as quick.

"Hey, you," he called out, pointing to me. "What are you pulling here?"

"We're waiting for Jerry's Aunt Irene to come to. We had nothing to do with your...demise."

"Demise! Cut the shit," he said, then suddenly floated up above his gurney, leaving his body behind. "What the hell is this? And why do you all look so fucked up. You're covered with scales. Like damn fish."

"So are you."

He lifted one of his arms and studied it. "Holy shit, you're right."

"And if you haven't noticed, you're flying. Bet you couldn't do that before you croaked."

"But I was just at the bar with Mike and Johnny. We were waiting for the fight to go on, tossing back a few. Maybe the nachos got me. I knew I was overdoing it but, man, were they good. Free nachos every Sunday and Wednesday. Benny's Bar on 14th Street. Cold Bud on tap, big screen TV, padded bar stools. I should have paid Benny rent."

"Never been there. I'm Henry. This is Jerry and Jennifer. And you are?"

"Richie Gold. I can't believe I'm dead."

"It's not so bad. And you're one of the lucky ones. Not everyone comes back after expiring."

"She's not here, Henry. Irene's not here!" Jerry said panicking.

"Are you sure?" I said, flying frantically from body to body, just like he and Jen were doing.

"I told you we shouldn't have gone home. They took her, Henry. They took Aunt Irene. Let's go upstairs and talk to Ed. Maybe he'll know where she is."

I turned to Richie. "Sorry, but we have to split. Don't worry, man, you're doing great."

"Easy for you to say."

"No work, no bills, no income tax, no rent increases." Richie lit up. "Hey, it's all good. We'll be back to see you." And we took off for the cafeteria.

Jerry spotted Big Ed and hurried over. "Ed, Irene's gone," he said, totally distraught.

"Did she have family, anyone who'd take care of the arrangements?" he asked. His spirit cohorts sitting around the table all commiserated. A live middle-aged man to the right of Ed ate a bowl of chili, unaware of the drama surrounding him.

"No, just me. It's been the two of us for years. Her husband died a long time ago; they never had kids."

"The state will step in, like they did for me. Cremation probably. It's cheaper. If she's got anything left, she'll find her way back. Probably show up at her apartment one of these days. Or she could head back here. We're the cafeteria spooks, but there are groups all over this place. Lots of people don't have anywhere to go, so they return to the last place they were. When they get back to Saint John's most of them like it, so they stay. At some point we're going to outnumber the living here."

We took the bus home in silence. Each of us secretly hoped to see Aunt Irene flying around when we got to her apartment. She wasn't, of course. Patience, that's what we needed now.

A couple of days later we made good on my promise to see how Richie Gold was doing. We entered the morgue to find him floating aimlessly about the dark frigid room.

"How's it going, Richie?" I said, happy to see him up and about. No one else was stirring.

"I'm bored shitless. Feels like I've been here a month, more maybe. And not one of these corpses has made a sound. Some of them get out of here almost as fast as they get in. They have family. I've got no one looking out for me. My wife tried to kill me once. We got loaded, only this time instead of just threatening, she stabbed me. The good news was we finally realized the marriage was over. Never married again."

"And I thought Maxine was bad."

"Hey, do you think I'll be stuck here much longer?"

"According to Ed, someone from the state will come soon. Hope you didn't have your mind set on a cushy cemetery burial because it'll probably be cremation."

"Hadn't thought about it. Hey, man, I'm only forty-nine. But heart problems run in the family. My father and grandfather; my mother's side wasn't much better. But when you think about it, you got to be nuts to choose to be trapped under the ground. Nah, cremation is fine with me."

"Where will you go after?"

Richie smiled. "That's easy. Benny's. The poor man's paradise. Come by sometime and I'll buy you a drink." He winked.

"No more drinking on this side," I said. "But we can still inhale weed."

"Never was into that, but if it's the only game in town, I'm in. Don't forget, come see me at Benny's. You can smell the beer, especially when they break open a new keg."

We flew to the cafeteria to see if Ed had seen Aunt Irene, but there'd been no sign of her. "She'll come around," he assured us. "Not to worry."

But that was like asking a bear to quit shitting in the woods.

Chapter 7
STOP TO SMELL THE ROSES

Every few days we went to Saint John's to see if Irene was there, but still no one had seen her. We continually expected her to turn up at the apartment; no luck there either. Jerry and Jennifer knew their days in his urn were numbered. New tenants would eventually move in and their urn would likely end up in a thrift store.

One fine afternoon we were sitting by the pool getting high with Larry and Greg. "No matter what I can't move out of that apartment. If I do I'm afraid Irene will come back and find only strangers living there." Jerry took a deep breath of smoke in, let it out and sighed.

"I understand, but doesn't it make more sense to move in with me and Pam? You can go to Irene's every day to see if she came back. Pam has a collection of mid-century glass. A lot of the pieces would make a good home for you and Jen."

"Nah, we got to stay put."

A couple of days later a Salvation Army truck pulled up in front of the building. Right away I knew Jerry and Jen were in trouble. I flew down to their apartment entering through the open balcony door. Jerry was in the living room lounging on Aunt Irene's yellow velvet sofa and watching television like he didn't have a care in the world.

"Jerry, I hate to tell you this, but I think you're screwed," I said.

"What are you talking about?" he asked, obviously stoned.

"Look outside."

Jerry half flew, half walked to the window in the kitchen that fronted on the street. "Beautiful day," he said.

"Jer, are you blind?"

"What are you talking about? Those guys over there?"

"Exactly. And look where they just came from."

"Where's that?"

"The truck, Jerry. For God's sake, don't you see the Salvation Army truck?"

"Yeah. So?"

"I think they may be here to cart Irene's stuff away."

"Jesus. Good thing Jen's at T.J. Maxx. I wouldn't want her seeing this."

The men, one tall Mexican and one short heavy-set white guy, entered the building, and in no time the door to Irene's apartment swung open. George, our obnoxious resident manager, led the way. We stood in the kitchen doorway facing the living room, frozen with fear.

"Take it all, guys. Don't leave anything behind," George said.

"This stuff is so out of style most of it will never sell. Some old stuff is okay, but this stuff is just ugly. Especially that couch," the short guy said.

"I'm glad Irene's not around to hear what they're saying. She loved her things," Jerry said sadly.

"You have to take it, all of it. Look, I give you guys a lot of business. Take the good with the bad. Hey, it's free and not that bad. The old lady kept everything in great shape. Some of it looks brand new. I think I'll take a couple of things myself. Give me a minute here." George walked around the room perusing the possibilities. As he neared the urn atop the end table Jerry and I became exponentially more frantic.

"Jesus," Jerry whispered. "I'll kill myself if I end up with George. He just may be the most annoying person I've ever met. And he always plays that damn rap music. Jen and I would lose our minds living with him."

I knew Jerry was right but held back from saying anything. It would only make the situation worse. But when George stood directly over the end table, our worst fears materialized. He picked up the urn, flipped open the lid, sniffed at the contents. We were no longer breathing. This truly was the end.

"Is this what I think it is?" he said.

"Yup. Someone's buried in there," the short guy said.

"Why do people keep this shit around? It's fucking ghoulish. Bury me ten feet under when I check out. I don't want my ashes on anybody's table. Can't stand the thought of it."

"Where I come from the dead are revered. The old lady who lived here loved whoever's inside there. It's okay by me," the Mexican mover said.

"Whatever," George said with disgust, tossing the urn onto the sofa. He lifted the table the urn had been on. "This table isn't so bad. I'll take it. You guys take the urn. I don't care what you do with it. Just get it out of here."

"Right, boss," and the short one wrapped the urn in a piece of newspaper and threw it into a packing box.

"How long do you think you'll be?" George asked, grabbing an ornate crystal candy dish filled with M & Ms on his way out the door.

"Couple of hours."

"I'll be in 110. Come by before you go and I'll sign the papers." The door slammed behind him.

"Jesus, Henry, I don't know what's worse. Ending up with George or winding up on a shelf in a Salvation Army store."

"You'll do fine without your urn and ashes," I said, trying to comfort him. "Plenty of dead people don't have them."

"I know, but it was home. Our minds are made up, though. As long as there's a chance Irene will come back, Jen and I are staying right here."

"I get it, buddy. And who knows, maybe some cool people will move in."

Jerry grinned. "Yeah. Cool people. That'll be cool. Maybe they'll be stoners. Then we won't always have to go to the pool. Speaking of which, what do you say we go there right now?"

"To smell the roses?"

"Yeah, what else? To smell the roses."

Chapter 8
HARLEY

Irene hadn't come back, but Jerry and Jennifer got a new roommate. Harley was batshit crazy, a certifiable lunatic. Aside from observing Harley, which Jerry, Jennifer and I had been doing with unwavering interest, we deduced this from a visit he had with Nicole, a twenty-something woman he apparently met while both were under treatment at a Beverly Hills mental facility.

She came over soon after he moved in. Instead of ringing the bell, she impatiently rapped on his door. He didn't open it right away, so she kept banging. It woke Jerry and Jennifer from an afternoon snooze and got me flying downstairs to see what the hell was going on. I saw a pretty blonde smashing both fists on Harley's door. She was smiling so I didn't think she had ill intent. Still, she could have been one of those thwarted angry women who slash tires and key cars when they think some guy's done them wrong. Of course that's never happened to me. Just saying. Anyway, finally he came to the door.

"Hey, Nicole. What's up?" he said.

"What took you so long, Trip?" Trip was her pet name for him. I assumed it was because he liked to travel.

Nicole strode into the apartment, slamming the door behind her. If there's one thing I could never stand it's apartment door slammers. If I could speak to the living I'd catch each and every one of them in the act and read them the riot act. Harley, I had to say, was no slammer, which may be because he didn't want to wake Sam who slept in the living room only yards from the front door. More about Sam later.

"Miss the old asylum?" Nicole asked.

"No way. Look what I've got going here. A veritable paradise. Just bought the TV at Best Buy. 65 inches," he said proudly.

"Good going, Trip. That's bigger than the one we had at Pleasant Hills. Better picture too. So how goes it? Been taking your meds?"

"When I feel like it. Mostly I'm sticking with medical marijuana. Works for me. How about you?"

She shook her head no, then smacked herself lightly on the forehead as if she had merely forgotten to stick to her prescribed regimen. Then she laughed maniacally. He joined her in kind. They kept it up for quite a while. None of us got the joke, but to them not taking medication was a real riot. "I'll have a toke if you've got any," Nicole said.

"That's like asking someone who rides around in an ice cream truck if he has any ice cream. Hey, remember the trucks with the bells? You're probably too young. Everyone came running when they got to your block and jingled. You know what, I should buy myself an ice cream truck, ride around the neighborhood and sell ice cream to stoners and little kids. I'd wear one of those white hats, white jacket too. It would have to be Good Humor ice cream though. I love Good Humor." He picked up a half-smoked joint from an ashtray on a table that looked like it was picked from the garbage. "Knock yourself out. Just had a whole doobie. I'm sufficiently stoned."

"Maybe you are getting better. Never heard you say you had enough."

"Mellowing with age."

"Think you'll have to go back to the Hills any time soon?"

"Hope not. I've had enough. Public hospitals, private rehab, when it comes down to it they're all the same. Jails with headshrinkers. I need to be free."

"Amen," Nicole said, taking a long hit. "To freedom for us lunatics," she said, toasting him with the joint. "You know what, Trip? Lunatics have rights too."

"You hear that, Sam? Lunatics have rights too. Hey, where are your manners? You forgot to say hello to Nicole." Harley was speaking to a stuffed bear who wore blue shorts, a yellow T-shirt and white Nikes, and was sitting on a chair facing the TV. Nicole apparently knew Sam from Pleasant Hills. "Hi, Sam," she said. "Don't you get tired of watching *Frozen*?"

As if all this wasn't enough to tip us off to Harley's mental state, we garnered additional info regarding his back story from his cell phone conversations as well as conversations he had with himself. Yes, a little talking to oneself is entirely fine, but hours spent conversing and debating solo are not. He also engaged in spirited conversations with his stuffed bear, the aforementioned Sam, who had more clothes than he did.

What we discovered was that Harley was originally from Miami Beach, spent years living in New York, did a long stint in Elmhurst General, a mental institute for LSD over-imbibers and the run-of-the-mill deranged. Harley fit neatly into both categories. It was there that Harley got stabbed in the stomach while saving a nurse from a fellow inmate who'd gone mad (well, madder). He was hailed a hero on the ward, then received permanent disability and a sizable settlement, enabling him to live a comfortably decent life should he ever leave the hospital. He moved to Los Angeles for the weather and a change of venue when he hit sixty. Jennifer, Jerry and I continued to scrutinize him like he was the meat of our doctoral dissertations.

The first day he moved in, the three of us had stood around in nervous anticipation. A red pickup truck parked in front of our building, and a male who didn't look old enough to have a driver's license and another who turned out to be Harley leapt out. For what seemed like an unusually long time, Harley stared at our building rubbing his hands together vigorously. "Man, this is going to be so cool. I love this place already. Hey, Tony, this looks like the building they filmed *Melrose Place*."

"What's that?"

"An old TV show. Okay, let's do it," and the two began hauling boxes and furniture into Irene's apartment. There wasn't much to haul.

We watched Harley bounce, not walk, as they dumped everything on the living room floor except for a king-sized mattress, which they dragged along the newly installed beige carpet into the bedroom. For a guy his age his agility and strength were impressive, and he obviously had been handsome when younger, still was. He had that chiseled kind of face, great features, a Warren Beatty type. And he still had hair, plenty of it, black streaked with silver, like it had been done in a salon only it wasn't.

"What do you think, Jerry?"

"Can't say for sure. What do you think, Jen?"

"Looks like he could have been a movie star."

"Don't get any ideas."

"Will you stay?" I asked.

"I haven't given up on Aunt Irene coming back, and he seems alright." Jerry, Jen and I kept watching Harley like he was a first-run movie. We were three proverbial flies on the wall, and the guy was mesmerizing.

Now this was before we knew how truly nuts he was. But even after we discovered his liabilities, Harley seemed to have a decent heart. Not much chance of him turning into a Craig's List murderer (he found the apartment on Craig's List) or a convert-to-Islam terrorist.

"I'm going to get a big screen TV like the one they had at the funny farm." Harley pointed to the longest wall in the living room. "It'll go right there."

That locked up the deal for Jerry. "We should stay, right Jen?" Jennifer smiled.

"I think we're done," he said to Tony, handing him a hundred dollar bill. "Couldn't have done it without you, man. Come by for a beer one of these days."

"Will do."

As soon as he thought he was alone he skipped from room to room, opening all the closets and cabinets, humming an indecipherable but catchy tune. He then doubled back to the living room, kneeled down and sliced open a box marked with a large black X on all four sides. We couldn't wait to see what was inside.

"Pictures," I guessed. "I bet it's pictures of his girlfriend or maybe his family."

"Something tells me he doesn't have family or any that he keeps in touch with. I'll go with girlfriend," Jerry said.

"Grass," Jennifer said excitedly. "He's a stoner for sure."

We watched as he pulled out a stuffed bear, the expensive kind you see advertised around the holidays that come with a life-long health guarantee and clothes, hats and shoes.

"You okay, Sam?" Harley seemed overly concerned about the bear's well-being. "I know it was a long haul, but this is it, buddy. We're home." And he placed Sam gently down on an ancient stuffed chair covered with a faded cabbage rose print that wouldn't look out of place in an alley. "The TV's going to be right there." And he pointed with a deranged grin on his face. "A HUGE one."

Sam appeared to nod, but maybe that was just my wishful thinking. Hey, I had a bear once.

Then the clincher came. He opened another box and took out five water pipes, an eclectic collection of small pipes, a couple of packs of Zig Zag and a baggie bulging with weed. He put all this paraphernalia on the white tiled kitchen counter, then proceeded to roll ten joints...perfectly. He put one between his lips and lit it with an expensive silver lighter engraved with the initials HM. He took a hit, then raised the joint high towards the kitchen window. "To my new abode."

Jerry smiled from ear to ear. "I'll second that." We flew over to sample Harley's stash.

Later that night, Jerry and Jennifer moved into one of Harley's water pipes, an old blue glass one he never uses that he keeps on a shelf in the dinette. Their scales vaporized into the darkness as the happy couple settled into their new home.

Chapter 9
NEW FRIENDS

Having the common sense of a toddler and a passion for good weed, Harley was a natural fit for Larry and Greg, who conveniently lived next door. What I didn't anticipate was Harley and Pam getting together.

Pam, a born do-gooder, couldn't turn her back on orphans, the infirm, the elderly, the environment, the homeless or any cause she deemed worthy. She worked as a physician's assistant, dispensing her very special brand of kindness to every patient who came her way. It wasn't unusual for Pam to receive high praise in Yelp reviews of the oncologist she worked for. She was one of those people who was tireless in their commitment to do good, so when a friend told her about a petition that would give Santa Monica residents a voice in future development, she enthusiastically volunteered to collect signatures to get the motion put on the ballot.

Stoner Ghosts of Santa Monica

She took the petition to work, and soon filled six pages with signatures. I thought she would be satisfied and hand her petitions in, but there was one more week until the deadline and against my better judgment, she decided to go around our building and ring doorbells. This, in my opinion, was a very bad idea. I didn't know everyone in the building, admittedly very few, but those I did know were stoners and womanizers, with at least one genuine lunatic on the tenant roster. It's one thing to say hello to these people when you pass them in the hallway or meet up with them in the laundry room; it's another thing entirely to enter their apartments. This was, after all, not the good old 1950s. Freaks, rapists, and terrorists abound everywhere. Few of us truly knew who we lived among. The only inhabitants I could vouch for in this building were Jerry and Jennifer, and they were dead. Larry and Greg were unquestionably of questionable character. Granted some of the good-looking struggling starlets were probably harmless, but how could you know who lived in which apartment? It was a real crap shoot when you rang a bell. There was no way I was able to convey this to Pam, who was all fired up to fill more petition pages. I'd attempted to enter her dreams the previous night to tip her off about the perils of canvassing our building but was unsuccessful; dream entry had been tough for me lately. So there was nothing left for me to do except shadow her from apartment to apartment. I planned on using some of my ghostly tricks if anyone tried anything; I'd attempt to scare the crap out of them, but that didn't always work either.

She got up one weekend morning raring to go. After her usual a.m. vegetable shake, she held fast to her clipboard and pen, shoved her house keys into the pocket of her jeans and exited our apartment. I followed closely behind. She started with the apartment next door, the scene of my ex-wife Maxine's demise and the place I used to live. I looked over Pam's shoulder half expecting to see my old nemesis and the beautiful mid-century furniture she robbed from me, but instead a young double for Marilyn Monroe opened the door. I'd never seen her before; she must have just moved in. The people in this building were constantly moving or changing roommates.

"Hi, I'm Pam, your neighbor. I'm collecting signatures..." and she continued with her spiel about ruthless builders and height variances. Marilyn agreed to sign and we quickly moved on to the next apartment. We covered the entire second floor, 12 apartments in all. We headed downstairs and my worries intensified. The first floor was where Larry and Greg lived, along with their friends Bob and Dave, who I often saw completely wasted at the pool but didn't really know. Truth was I stuck mostly with my own kind, the dead ones, and of course with Pam who I adored. It hit me that Harley also lived on the first floor. As far as I knew Pam and Harley's paths had yet to cross. I worried that after meeting him she might view him as another cause, adding mentally ill to her list of those worthy of her help. I wasn't sure if she had much experience in the deranged department. The thought of her hanging out with Harley did not sit well with me. True she'd realize right off that he was screwy, but he looked like a movie star. This was a potentially problematic combination, though I did give Pam credit for having good sense...well, for the most part. After all, she did fall for me.

We were near the end of our expedition, with only two apartments to go. Pam rang Larry and Greg's bell. She waited, then rang again. Apparently the two were out somewhere, probably buying weed and beer for the weekend. I wished there was some way for me to stop her from ringing Harley's bell. There wasn't. I stood close by her side, scales flickering with energy, as she rang his bell. There was a chance he wasn't home, a chance he didn't feel like answering the bell, a chance he was in an inebriated sleep. I was trying to dredge up other possible scenarios when the door abruptly opened. Harley stood leaning against the doorframe a huge smile on his face.

His eyes were red and watery but wide open; there was no question he was lit.

"Hey," he said.

She hesitated just a beat. His looks may have surprised her, but she quickly rebounded into her practiced talk. "I'm your neighbor, Pam. I live upstairs." She pointed up as if he couldn't figure out where upstairs might be. "I'm collecting signatures to give Santa Monica..."

"You know something?" he cut her off but didn't wait for her to ask what. "You could be Nicole's mother. You look just like Nicole. Man, it's crazy. You don't have a daughter named Nicole, do you?"

"No, I never had children."

"Me neither. Not that I know of, anyway." He laughed. His teeth were snowy white against the perfect light tan of his face. They must hand out tooth whitener in Beverly Hills loony bins. How was she going to resist this guy? My only hope was that he would do something psycho and fast.

Pam cleared her throat, then tried to continue where she left off. "It's especially important for renters to..."

"I like you," he said, interrupting again. I looked into the apartment to see if Jerry or Jen were around for back-up, but there was no sign of them. He was beginning to look like a homicidal maniac to me, but Pam didn't seem the least bit concerned.

"It's weird," he went on. "I feel like I know you."

"No, I don't think so," she said, her free hand playing with a strand of her long blonde hair. When a woman did this, I knew it was a sign of something, but couldn't remember exactly what.

"Yeah, I guess it's probably just you looking like Nicole's mom."

"Who's Nicole?"

"A friend of mine. I met her at Pleasant Hills."

"Oh, that's nice," Pam said, likely thinking Pleasant Hills was a yoga retreat or posh resort. She stared at Harley. "You know something really funny? You remind me of someone, too."

I held my breath. Was she going to say Bill Owen, the geeky guy she dated in college before me who ended up making a mint on Wall Street? Or maybe her deceased husband who's buried back in Queens? "Who?" he asked, grinning.

"My boyfriend at NYU." I was right, he reminded her of Bill, that dickface. I didn't like the fact that she remembered him at all. Bill, or William as he made everyone call him once he hit it big, ended up with a townhouse in Greenwich

Village and a spread in the Hamptons. "His name was Henry."

My heart soared and sunk simultaneously. I was happy she was thinking about me but concerned that this feeling of familiarity could turn disastrous. And just what did she think this psycho and I had in common anyway?

"The one who got away, huh?" he said.

"Kind of. But he's living with me now."

"Oh." Harley sounded disappointed.

"Henry's dead. His ashes are in an urn on my dresser. We talk though. Everyday. And sometimes I dream about him." I hate to admit this, but if anyone else were listening, Pam was sounding somewhat unhinged herself.

"Yeah, I talk to my mom a lot. Didn't see enough of her when she was alive, but she's with me now. I'll sign," he said, changing the subject.

Pam handed him the clipboard and a pen. He started to write his name, but the pen had run out of ink. "I've got one in the kitchen. Come on in."

Harley sounded way too much like the wicked witch in *Little Red Riding Hood*. I was totally horrified. I hoped Pam had the sense to stay right where she was, but I wasn't betting on it.

"Sure," she said, and glided into his apartment. The wind slammed the door shut behind her. Thankfully I flitted in just before it closed. She stood in the living room while Harley went into the kitchen and came out holding a pen. He made a flourish of signing his name and writing his address. "There you go," he said, and handed the clipboard back to her.   "You busy? Sam and I were just going to watch *Frozen.*"

Well now, things were definitely looking up. Sam was the ticket to Pam discovering just how nuts her newfound friend was.

"Yours is the last apartment I have to do, and I've been meaning to see why everyone likes that movie so much."

"Great," he said, and she followed him over to his couch, black leather with several slashes on the cushions. Sam sat on the crack in the middle wearing a flowered dress and matching sun bonnet. Harley flopped down to the left of Sam and patted the couch on Sam's other side. "Sit. It's pretty comfortable. I got it really cheap at the Salvation Army because there's tears in it. Oh, and this," he patted Sam's furry leg, "is Sam."

"Hello, Sam," Pam said, exhibiting no indication that she found it the least bit odd that she had been introduced and was speaking to a stuffed bear.

My worst fears were realized; I was so fucked.

Chapter 10
TRIPPING WITH TRIP

It was morning and judging from the position of the sun in the cloudless sky, fairly early. I was an early riser, always had been. Jerry too. Jennifer was still asleep in Harley's bong, same as she loved to do when she was alive. Sometimes Jerry and I met at the pool before she got up to shoot the breeze, but today Harley's old blue convertible was parked right in front of the building; its white (now more like gray) top was down, giving us easy access onto the back seat. At some point in this car's life it must have been a beauty but passing years and Harley had taken their toll. The exterior was all banged up, the result, I was certain, of Harley driving under the influence, and the inside was loaded with trash, mostly food and beverage containers (another direct result of his stoner ways, fast food, M & M's and ice cream being perennial pothead favorites).

Jerry bent over and sniffed at a Jack in the Box bag. "Chicken Fajita Pita," he proclaimed, then opened the bag to see if he was right. "I just can't miss," he said, holding out the bag. "See."

Grooving in the sunlight under the swaying palms in the now quiet streets, I asked, "What should we do today?" But before he had time to answer, Harley leapt up and over into the driver's seat. Then Nicole came slinking towards the car. Before she starts talking she could be mistaken for one of the pretty wannabe actresses in our building. I would have gone for her myself back in the day. I fully underestimated the importance of mental health, stability and personality in a mate then, as so many of us did and still do. Saying some chick had a good personality was like giving her the kiss of death in the dating world.

Nicole entered the car using the passenger door. "I'm dying for a cinnamon roll. Can't think of anything else since I got up this morning," Harley said, starting the car. The engine coughed a few times, then kicked in. "We're off." And before Jerry or I could even think to make a run for it, we were heading down Fourth Street.

"Jesus. Cinnamon buns. Haven't had one since I don't know when," Jerry said wistfully.

"Smell much?"

"Fresh out of the oven they can't be beat. Where do you think Harley's going?"

I leaned back in the seat, wind whipping my scales. "It doesn't matter. It's not like we have to get to work."

"Yeah, you're right."

Harley lit a joint and passed it to Nicole. "We're always on the same page," she said, taking a couple of hits.

No way to refute that. A pity two such great-looking people were so mentally impaired. Then again, who doesn't have something wrong with them?

"With all this wind I can't catch any of their smoke," Jerry said.

"At the lights, Jer. There'll be plenty of opportunities."

By the time Harley swung onto the 405 all four of us were pretty toasted.

"Where's he going?" Jerry asked, his hands attempting to keep his scales from hitting him in the face.

"No clue. You'd think he could find some buns on Wilshire."

The radio was blasting classic rock and Harley was chugging along in the right-hand lane. "He'll probably exit anytime now," I said. "Maybe he knows a place in the Valley."

The wind made conversation difficult, so I sung along to the songs on the radio. Amazing how I could remember the words to almost every old song but couldn't recall anything about

American or world history. And what about algebra and geometry? It's like all those classes never happened. "Like a Rolling Stone" came on and I sung every word.

We were stuck in traffic on the 101 passing through Encino. I figured he'd pull off the freeway the next exit or two. At least when we slowed down in heavy traffic the wind let up.

"Where are we going, Trip?" Nicole asked, after emitting a cloud of smoke, some of which we were able to inhale as we leaned forward. I never cared much for convertibles, thought they were overrated. Sure they look great, but I couldn't stand the wind. It really messed my hair up, which wasn't my best attribute to begin with; when I started losing it, the problem grew exponentially. The few times I rode in anyone's convertible I insisted on keeping all the windows up. No surprise, the windows were down in Harley's car. No doubt he loved wind smacking him in the face, and his hair looked especially striking flowing behind him, silver streaks gleaming in the sun. Man, what I would have done for hair like that.

Harley steered the wheel with his left hand, as he sang along to "Nowhere Man." He kept his right hand available for joint holding. "Hey, Trip, did you hear me? Where are we going? I've got an appointment with my shrink in Westwood at five."

144

"We'll make it back, no problem."

Nicole lit up another joint and passed it to Harley. We all got a fresh buzz going, and no one seemed to care where we were headed or when we'd get there. Ah, yes, "Nowhere Man," indeed.

We passed through the beautiful enclaves of Santa Barbara and Montecito. I read the freeway signs and watched farmland go by, no cares. If I weren't stoned I'd have been freaked out about driving this far with Harley. Even short trips were problematic when he was at the helm. Jerry appeared to be passed out, which was probably a very good thing. Jen would wonder where we were, and he'd worry about that. In any case, Harley drove on.

I must have nodded off, because suddenly he was exiting the freeway. Clearly I'd missed a bunch of signs and now had no idea where we were. The town we were driving through looked like it was the 1950s all over again. The streets were lined with small houses and old-fashioned stores and restaurants; no mini mansions, no buildings taller than three stories. A few blocks ahead the ocean shimmered under the sunlight. It was odd that a beach town kept its original character and hadn't been attacked by tasteless builders successful in creating their homogenous landscapes. There wasn't a

McDonalds or Starbucks in sight. Where the hell were we?

Harley pulled along the curb and came to a stop in front of a block of shops. Parking spots for the taking and no meters! I expected to see Rod Serling pop out of a doorway to announce that we'd entered the *Twilight Zone*. But it was only Harley who popped excitedly out of the car. "Nicole, this is it. Pismo Beach. Damn, we should move here."

"I've never been here, but it looks kind of, hmmm, funky. Maybe not in such a good way."

"I was only here once, passing through on the way to Hearst Castle. Man, that was a trip and a half. Ever go there?" She shook her head. "That rich newspaper guy owned it. It was his house. A huge, and I mean huge, mansion. What a pool. My friend Harvey and I got wrecked and went on the tour. Then we spent the night at the Madonna Inn in a room with rock walls, even in the shower; it was supposed to be a cave. The place had a big ballroom downstairs and old people came all dressed up for a dance. It was a hoot. Anyway, I fell in love with Pismo first time I laid eyes on it. We were making a bathroom stop and happened upon this unbelievable place for cinnamon rolls. Just wait, you'll see."

Nicole looked skeptical, but followed him into a large, old-fashioned, shabby restaurant. Old West Cinnamon Rolls was printed in big white block letters on the glass storefront. Jerry and I followed them inside. There was a counter and a glass showcase with an impressive display of buns clearly labeled: plain, frosted, raison, almond, pecan, crumb. They were lined up neatly in big rectangle aluminum pans. Jerry looked like he wanted to fly around to the other side and jump right in.

"What'll you have, Nic?" he asked.

"Plain. And a cup of coffee."

A woman with a genuine smile took Harley's order. "One plain, two with frosting, one pecan and two with crumbs."

"You're going to get fat, Tripster."

"Worth it," he said, handing the pleasant woman a twenty. "Heat one plain, one frosted, and one crumb, and put the rest in a box to go. Oh, and one coffee, one water. Please." He turned to Nicole. "My mother taught me to always say please. Thank you, too. She was real big on that."

They sat at a table by the window, and slowly ate their buns with a plastic knife and fork. "Ah, life is grand, isn't that so?" Harley said, slicing into his crumb bun.

"I have to admit I've never had a cinnamon bun this good before. It's worth the trip, Trip."

"I knew you'd think so."

Jerry seemed consumed with the smell of the coffee mixed with an avalanche of cinnamon.

I was enjoying myself but hoping that in this idyllic spot Harley would realize that Nicole was not only his mentally deficient buddy and fellow drug abuser, but that he was in love with her. That would put an end to any worries I harbored about him getting together with Pam. But they just ate their buns in contented silence. After they finished, we flew along as they walked down to the pier. Harley actually skipped, and Nicole kept up with him by increasing her pace. I rooted for them to hold hands. It didn't happen.

They stopped at the entrance to the wooden pier and looked out at the ocean. Awesome view; mountains to the left and right, dogs and children and their parents on the beach and in the water, surfers in wetsuits riding the waves. It would make a perfect picture postcard. That is until a group of older women stopped beside us, each with a very small dog on a leash.

"Wow, look at all these dogs," Nicole said, kneeling down to pet a white one. "What a face. So beautiful."

"Rachel's a show dog," her owner said with pride. "Long-coat Chihuahua. We did a show yesterday in Paso Robles. Rachel was a winner. So were Farrah and William." She pointed to two of the other dogs. As if his name was a cue, William, a tiny black and white, began yapping like mad at Jerry, who stood just inches away. Jerry retreated, but William pulled forward on his leash in a demonic burst of strength, all five pounds of him. It made me laugh until the little fucker started coming at me. We both sprinted out of his range, but that didn't stop his tirade, and then Farrah, Rachel and four others joined in. The gaggle of pipsqueak privileged pups had segued into a pack of virulent, pulsating, multi-colored hair. Even previously timid Prince Charles, the last mannerly holdout, had chosen to turn against me and my buddy in a vicious display of bad dog temper. For all their excessive breeding, training and fluffing they were now no better than a common pack of street strays.

The women frantically tried to quell the uprising with little success. "What's gotten into Prince Charles?"

"Farrah has never made so much as a peep."

Rachel's owner turned to her friends. "It must be that blue brindled fawn Maxwell from Los Angeles. Such a poor influence on the others. Did you see how he tried to rile Rachel while she was being groomed, sniffing at her privates and barking incessantly? It was beyond rude. But my girl held her composure. If you ask me, it took much too long for Maxwell's owner to finally drag that awful dog away." She looked at Nicole, who stood several yards from the foaming canines. "This is so out of character for Rachel. She never barks. That's the first thing you must teach them when you train them to show. No barking. But not to worry, we'll remedy the problem in no time." She snatched Rachel up, who continued to yap and snarl in my direction.

Nicole smiled and nodded her head in sympathy, then looked down at her watch. "It's getting late. We should start back. We have a long trip."

"Okay, let's shove off. It's 12:30; we'll make it back by four. Have a fine day, ladies," Harley said. The barking receded as we quickly made our way back to the car.

Chapter 11
A FLY ON THE WALL,
A SPOOK ON THE FLOOR

At Jerry's insistence, we were at Saint John's again looking for Aunt Irene. Personally I thought there was no chance she was coming back. The way I saw it, she never came to (another of the dead dead) or she got hung up at the crematorium. I'd heard that happened fairly often. Cremas were a hotbed of homeless fliers.

We got to the cafeteria and sure enough there was Ed and his bunch sitting at their usual table, only this time a few more deceased had joined them. "Hi, Ed, how you doing?" Jerry said in greeting, anxious to get to the point.

Big Ed looked up and smiled. "Ed, I was wondering if you've seen a new woman around here. She's in her nineties, thin, long gray hair? My Aunt Irene. Remember, you helped us find her in the emergency room?"

"Yeah, sure, I remember. Let me think." Ed rubbed his scaly fingers over his chin and paused. "You know what? She may be down in radiation."

"Why would anyone want to go there?"

"It's a swell spot. One of the best waiting rooms anywhere. Huge windows, bright as all get out cause of the southern exposure, plenty of comfy chairs and sofas. Same magical light as New Orleans back when my boys and I did cover for Skynyrd on Frenchmen Street. What a time that was. Now what was I saying? Oh, radiation. If it wasn't for the food," he gazed at the counter bins filled with fried chicken, mashed potatoes, gravy and biscuits, "I would've holed up there myself. Let's go have a look see."

We made the trip down and after waiting for someone to open the door, entered a light-filled room. There were a few live patients awaiting treatment but even more, many, many more, spooks all around the room. They were talking and laughing and acting as if they were having the time of their lives, like they were at a wedding or high school reunion.

"Who would have thought?" I said, thoroughly blown away.

"I think that's her. In front of the window," and Jerry hurried off in her direction.

He came to a quick stop in front of a row of fliers seated in chairs, their backs the beneficiary of the warm late morning sun streaming through the windows. "Irene! It's me. Jerry."

"Oh, my Lord," she said, her scaly face breaking into a big smile. "Jerry. What a wonderful surprise."

Jerry kneeled in front of her. "I've been waiting for you to come back home, Aunt Irene. I was worried about you. Why didn't you go back to your apartment?"

"I'm so sorry you worried, but I didn't know what to do or where to go when I suddenly came to at the crematory. I never expected anything like that to happen, never was one who believed in an afterlife. So you were in my apartment all those years? My Lord, I had no idea, no idea at all. I never heard a sound from you, never saw a sign. I thought you were gone like everyone else I ever knew who died, that the only thing left was your ashes. If I had known..."

"That's okay. We're together now." Jerry smiled like his long shot just won by a nose at the track.

The scales on Irene's face turned pink. "There's something else. I met someone at the crematory. Fred." Irene smiled girlishly. We hadn't noticed him before, but there was a dapper looking duffer sitting to her right. He waved hello.

"Oh," Jerry said.

"Fred and I were born the same year, 1923. The same month too. He thought we should go back to the hospital, said that made the most sense."

"It was a good start, anyway. Maybe not where we would end up, but someplace familiar. My wife died many years ago, and the children, well, they're not children anymore, live back east. No getting back there." Fred took Irene's scaly hand in his.

"We flew all around the hospital searching for the perfect place for us. We both love the sun so much, the minute we walked in here we knew it was home." Irene looked at Fred adoringly.

"Aunt Irene, I'm happy you're happy. But I thought if I ever found you, you'd come back home."

"Are you still in the apartment?"

"I stayed because I thought you'd be back."

"Who lives there now?"

"Well..." Jerry hesitated, still holding out hope Irene would return, maybe even bring Fred with her. That is, unless she found out the truth about Harley. She might be able to handle a nutter, but a pothead was another matter entirely for someone of her generation.

"Jerry, I know you too well. You're hiding something. Who's living there now?"

"A single guy just turned sixty. Moved here to, uh, retire. I'm not sure what he did before, but I know he traveled a lot. He likes to vacuum. A couple of times a day sometimes. He keeps the place real clean. Oh, and George put in new carpet. Beige. New linoleum in the kitchen and bathroom too. And new blinds. Looks great."

"And?" Irene asked.

"Well, I guess you could say Harley's a bit screwy, but everyone has problems, right?"

Ed chimed in. "I knew a fellow named Harley. Back in New York. He was always a little off, but then he took a mess of LSD and flipped his bird. It was the sixties so it wasn't that unusual, but they said if you had mental problems before you took LSD, it could really take you over the edge. I was there once when he got high. We were at a friend's apartment in Queens. If memory serves me, his name was Joel. Anyway, a bunch of us took a tab; it was Sandoz acid, the real deal. Harley took two. After maybe ten minutes he says it's not working and takes a third. We were all just hanging out, and it starts to come on. Real slow at first, then quick as a jetliner. We were blitzed, sitting round and talking about how cool everything looked under the influence, watching our faces morph into skeletons and such. Pretty mellow, harmless stuff until Harley announced he could fly. Before we could stop him he took off full throttle out a second story window. Broke both legs and an arm. Lucky it wasn't his neck. After he healed up, well, physically anyhow, they put him in a mental ward. In those days they could do that, you know, force you into a bughouse. It was the last I heard of old Trip."

I was on full alert. This was Harley he was talking about, the lunatic the love of my life was hanging with. "That's him! The guy Jerry and Jennifer live with. Trip. I thought they called him that because he traveled a lot."

"Well I'll be," Ed said, southern accent thickening. Just then I got a flash of Ed on stage in NOLA, long crazy blonde hair flowing as he whipped his guitar around and sang "Sweet Home Alabama."

"Sounds like it's him," Jerry said.

Irene looked at Fred; Fred looked at Irene. She hesitated before speaking. "I know you mean well, Jerry, but Fred and I are going to stay here. We're comfortable, all set up. A move for us at this point would be difficult. We do so appreciate your offer and hope you'll come and visit us often."

I sensed Jerry's disappointment, but he said, "Sure, I understand. I'll come every week."

"Do you think he's dangerous?" I asked Ed, getting right to the point. My point, that is.

"I don't really know, but I guess with folks like that you can never be sure."

"Jerry, we have to keep Pam away from him."

"Honestly, Henry, we haven't seen Harley do anything wrong and neither have you. Pam comes over, they watch TV, eat some snacks he puts out, chips and dips mostly. Sam's on the couch between them. Sure he's nuts, but I don't think Pam's in any danger. It must be hard seeing her with someone else, but the only move Harley ever makes is on Sam. You see how he likes to rub that bear's leg. But no one's seen him touch Pam, including you."

What he said was true, but still I felt unsettled. I didn't want to be a fly on his wall anymore. Trouble was I couldn't stop myself.

* * *

I followed Pam to Harley's apartment whenever she went there. It killed me to see him so happy to see her. Couldn't he find his own girl? He should start hitting on Nicole. Lots of women go for older men, and the guy has some bucks, though you'd never know it judging from his furniture. But Nicole hardly ever came around anymore, and when she did they just smoked and ate whatever was in his refrigerator and snack cabinet. He wasn't much of a grocery shopper, so the pickings were generally slim.

Yeah, nothing may have happened between them yet, but I was certain it was only a matter of time. Any day Harley would make his move and my beautiful Pam would fall hard for his good looks and mental disabilities.

One afternoon I sat on the kitchen counter and watched as Pam cooked up a big load of sausage and peppers. I figured she was having company, a friend over for dinner. Diane, a co-worker of hers, often came over. Pam cooked, Diane brought wine, and they'd shoot the breeze. Girl talk, except not much of it was about the men in their lives, at least not men who were currently alive. Diane also lost her husband, and both of them no longer dated. This didn't stop my relentless pursuit of weeding out any information regarding a possible hookup between Pam and Harley.

That night Diane never showed. Instead Pam put half the sausage and peppers in plastic containers in her freezer, placed a cover over what was left in the pot, then went into the bathroom. She put lipstick on, combed her hair, then went into the bedroom and changed into a pink T-shirt, which I found to be too tight, and a pair of jeans (ditto for tight). I didn't like where this seemed to be headed.

I followed her back into the kitchen. She grabbed her keys from a wall hook, stashed them in her pocket, picked up the pot and headed out the door. I knew exactly where she was going.

Down on the first floor she rang Harley's bell. He answered almost instantly. "What took you so long?" he asked, smiling and looking old movie star handsome.

"You can't rush sausages," my girl said, walking into his apartment. The door slammed before I could get in.

I panicked and slumped onto the hall floor to ruminate. Loud music played. I strained to hear their conversation, but it was hopeless. It was the Doors, but even Jim couldn't change my foul mood. I got up and flew around the corner to Harley's balcony. Maybe he'd left the slider open; he usually did. But I was royally screwed. The slider was shut tight, tight as her jeans, tight as her shirt. And the blinds were closed, too. I headed back to the hall. I sank down against the wall directly facing his door, my thoughts driving me crazy. I could've easily ended up in a nuthouse myself if they had one for spooks. Time passed; I had no idea how much. It seemed long, longer than any man should have to endure when his girl was with another man behind closed doors. I attempted to meditate but should have known better. It never worked for me before, why would it now?

Jerry and Jennifer flew over. "Henry, why are you sitting on the floor?" Jennifer said.

"It's Pam," I said, breathlessly. "She's in there...with him."

"It'll be alright. Nothing's ever happened before. No worries," Jerry said, patting the tingling scales on my arm.

"Easy for you to say, man. She made him sausage and peppers."

"Oh," Jennifer said, not daring to say another word. Women, man, they can read between the lines.

Chapter 12
WHAT'S GOING ON?

It was easy for Jerry and Jennifer to see I was driving myself mad. Now Jim was singing "Love Me Two Times." It was enough to kill me all over again. I remembered feeling the same way back in high school after Renee Linden broke up with me and I ran into her with Dave Brandt, the school quarterback, a week later at the movies. I spotted them sitting two rows in front of me. I don't think they saw me, but I had a first rate shot of them. Sharing popcorn, holding hands; the worst was when he snuck some side breast. And she didn't shake his hand off right away. It took me more than a month to get that far with her. To watch them you would have thought they'd been going out for years, but I was the one she went with. For eight months. I know this only because Renee made me take her to Jahn's Ice Cream Parlor to share a hot fudge sundae every month on the fifteenth to celebrate. So right off my friend Steve said we should leave. But not me, even then I was a glutton for punishment. I didn't see a minute of the movie, don't even remember which one it was, but I didn't miss a minute of the Renee and Dave show. I stayed glued to my seat the whole time, only turned around when the movie ended, hoping they wouldn't recognize the back of my head. We waited in our seats until everyone was gone and someone began sweeping the floor. Finally we got up. I'd had my fill; I didn't want to see them under the marquee lights all happy and shit.

When I got home that night I didn't sleep a wink; by morning I'd had an epiphany. That would never happen to me again. I would be the one to do the leaving; I would never care that much again. It wasn't always easy, but I got the hang of it for the most part. When I'd catch myself liking someone too much, I'd force myself to go out with someone else. Cheating, I rationalized, wasn't wrong: it was survival. When Pam and I got together in college, I fell pretty hard. But before it could get out of hand, I began screwing Susan Segal and a couple of other nameless chicks. Got away with it for a while until Pam caught me. A couple of times. In the beginning she let it fly, but then she called it quits. Even then I knew I'd lost the wrong one, a good one. But I wasn't about to change, not even for her. Three marriages, multiple affairs, one-nighters and countless screw-bys followed. I never got hurt again. Until now.

"C'mon, Henry, let's go to the pool. We have to give them time to eat. We won't miss anything," Jerry said, pulling me to my feet.

"I don't know," I said, eyes peeled to Harley's door. "People Are Strange" was coming through loud and clear.

"We'll get a few hits to relax, then come back."

Jennifer was silent, her expression one of concern. I worried she was worried about what was taking place inside that apartment too, only she wasn't saying. Women see things men can't, and that never changes, not even when they're dead.

Larry and Greg and a couple of other dopers were at a table drinking Coronas and passing joints. We hovered at low altitude above them, taking it all in. A flimsy veil of weed cloaked my anxieties; they weren't gone, only slightly averted. But by the time we got back to continue our vigil at Harley's door, they returned in full force. Only I was sleepy. I had no idea of the time, no idea how long Pam and Harley had been holed up inside, but it felt late. The door slamming in the building was down to a minimum; everyone had either gone out for the night or was hunkered down inside their apartment. Intermittent slamming would start up when people staggered home. I looked over at Jerry and Jen. They were on the floor leaning against one another, eyes closed. I thought I'd never sleep, not until Pam came out. But what if she didn't? What if she stayed the night? What then? If only I could speak to her, talk some sense into her. The guy was a lunatic. Nothing good could come of this. I only wanted what all guys want when they're crazy for a chick; I wanted her to wait for me. Yeah, I was dead, but that made no difference. We would hook up again at some point, I was sure of it. But if she and Harley hit it off, what chance did I have? He'd be the one she wants, the one she goes back to after she passes. No, they can't get together, they can't get together. I repeat this over and over like a mantra, but mantras don't work for me, as you know.

The door opened and Pam walked out of Harley's apartment. She carried a Ralphs paper grocery bag. The pan was inside; it was clean and empty. Harley stood in the doorway, a big smile on his face. She turned around to face him, then leaned in and they kissed. It was a long one, not a short friendly peck. I watched this from my floor vantage point. I saw everything. He ran his hands up and down the sides of her breasts. This seemed uncomfortably familiar. Deja vu. I was slumped in a movie theater seat again. This time it was Pam and Harley in front of me, only a few inches away. I could smell Pam's hair, the shampoo she always used. I was lost in her scent when George, the building manager, walked by. It was light out. Morning. Birds sang.

"What the hell are you doing in here?" he said to me. I opened my mouth to speak but nothing came out. I didn't understand; George could never see me before. "You!" he pointed in my direction. "Get the hell out of here. There's no homeless allowed in my building."

I didn't budge. I couldn't. I seemed to be stuck to the floor. I couldn't remember becoming homeless, but apparently I was. I felt hungry like I hadn't eaten in a real long time, hungry and cold. "If you don't get up I'm calling the cops." George was screaming now. A couple of people came out of their apartments to see what was happening. They were all looking down at me. The shame was overwhelming. I felt like a caged animal in a zoo. I wanted so much to get up and fly away. They'd be shocked, all of them. Shocked I could fly. "I'm not homeless," I wanted to shout, but I wasn't sure it was true. George got closer. I thought he was going to do something to me. I forgot about Pam and Harley. I was too afraid of what George was going to do.

A door clicked open. I heard Harley say, "The sausages were awesome. You're a super cook, Pam." His loud nutter voice woke me from a deep sleep and a horrifying nightmare.

"Thanks, I try."

Jerry and Jennifer were still fast asleep. I nudged them awake. "The door's open," I said. "Hurry." They rushed inside just before Harley shut it.

I followed behind Pam as she walked up the stairs to her apartment. She opened the door and fast as lightning I zipped in before she was even inside. I didn't want to be homeless, not even for one night.

I'm not homeless, I said aloud, as I vaporized and settled deep inside my urn. It was only a dream, right? A bad dream. Yeah, of course, just a bad dream. But then it hit me. I didn't know what had gone on with Pam and Harley besides eating sausages and peppers and listening to the Doors. This was my last thought as I fell exhausted into a welcome and thankfully dreamless sleep.

Chapter 13
OBSESSION

I was obsessed. I'd been down this road before. Maybe I've already mentioned it, but I have a touch of OCD. Well, okay, more than that, but sometimes I could go months without a major flare-up. And aside from acute anxiety accompanied by out-of-control whirling thoughts that my ex-wife Maxine was coming to move back in with me (and that's not crazy at all when you think about it), things had been cool since my death. No interminable hand washing which could easily morph into hand wringing when deceased, no gas jet stove checking or excessive wall and floor tapping-by-the-number. But what was happening to me now was equally debilitating. I'd become fixated on Pam and Harley and could think of little else. Jennifer tried to help, but so far our sessions had come to nothing.

I listened in on Pam's phone calls, certain that any minute she'd tell someone she had a new boyfriend. So far, nothing. When Diane came over for dinner one night, I positioned myself between them on one of Pam's four steel-framed dining chairs; they had striped, period-correct seat cushions. Pam made sausage and peppers, triggering a shitload of post-traumatic stress my way. I felt sick to the stomach I no longer possessed. I studied her face each time she spoke, then turned to Diane and focused in on her. I sought out clues, tells, back story. If I was a woman, I'd be able to read between their lines. My scaly head bobbed side to side like I was at a tennis match, but I got no pleasure from watching them.

"Dr. Jonas is going on vacation the last two weeks in June. Have you made plans to go away?" Diane asked.

Pam seemed to hesitate before answering, or maybe it was just my mania. Had she already planned a getaway with Harley? "Not yet. It's been awhile since I've gone anywhere," she said, taking a sip of wine.

I waited for her to continue, but she didn't. Except for a discussion about the sausages, which were Johnsonville, something I had absolutely no interest in knowing, and San Marzano tomatoes (ditto for lack of interest), I came away with no info except that these were ingredients that Chef Curtis Stone used. Then it occurred to me that Pam was hiding the truth from Diane. I became hopeful that after more wine she'd open up, but that didn't happen.

Unfortunately, Pam was never much of a drinker. The night ended before she proclaimed her love for her lunatic downstairs neighbor. Probably decided to keep her office and love life separate; perhaps she thought Diane was a yenta.

The next morning I followed Pam to the farmer's market. She bought tomatoes, broccoli, lettuce, cucumbers, brussel sprouts, asparagus and grapes. She didn't talk to anyone except the farmers she bought from. She smiled a lot though. A dead giveaway for the love struck, smiling for no apparent reason. But there was no fooling me. I knew exactly what she was thinking about: Harley, the dashing psychopath. He not only was Pam's latest project, she'd fallen in love with him. Who could resist those perfect white teeth and salon-looking hair? I'd always wanted hair like his. Reminded me of Don Johnson's, except Harley's was dark with streaks of silver. Yeah, not even gray, freaking silver. And it flowed in a breeze. The little I had left at the end tufted up around my head. Luckily scales covered my bald head now.

As I was strolling the sunny aisles behind her it occurred to me that she was planning to make dinner for Harley again. That's why she was buying more produce than usual. But the guy didn't eat vegetables or anything remotely healthy; Cheerios and bologna sandwiches were his go-to dinner staples. Broccoli and brussel sprouts had no place in his life. Not unless Pam was trying to convert him to her ways! Now that made perfect sense. She was attempting to healthy him up. Oh, was I screwed.

That night I hung around the apartment, following wherever she went. After eating a dinner of raw vegetables and humus, she watched a movie on television. It was the old James Bond flick, *Goldfinger*. It hit me instantaneously. That was the movie that was playing the disastrous night with Renee and the quarterback. This was a very bad omen. I couldn't remember the movie at all, having never watched a minute of it, but the song lyrics, "Goldfinger, the man with the Midas touch, a spider's touch," reached deep into my psyche. And that singer's ominous tone was nothing short of lethal. I would have collapsed onto the floor if I wasn't already sprawled out on the couch. I dared not look at the screen and put my hands over where my ears once were. I hummed loudly attempting to drown out all traces of that godawful song.

At long last the movie was over. Seemed to me she must have played it twice. Pam clicked the TV off and went into the bathroom. I was too stricken to follow, but realized I'd gotten through the night without her being with Harley. I flew into my urn totally spent. Pam came into the room, turned off the light and got into bed. If only things could stay like this, just the two of us in this room for eternity, I'd be cured of DSM 300.3 (Obsessive Compulsive Disorder). I supposed I qualified for DSM 300.2, Generalized Anxiety, as well.

When I woke the next day she'd already left for work.

There was no reason to follow her to her job, giving me time off from constant agitation. Much of my free time was now spent at the pool. There was usually at least one stoner around. Okay, I admit it, I'd been self-medicating way more than usual. But what could I do, take up bike riding? Wow, there was a thought. I could catch a ride with someone passing on the street. He or she would have no way of knowing I was hanging on behind them as they headed to Palisades Park or any one of many scenic destinations around here. And though it struck me as a tricky maneuver, I was stoned enough to attempt it. It was a warm sunny morning or afternoon, not certain which. I rushed outside, stood on California Avenue, and waited to hitch a ride. A man who appeared to be about the age I would have been rode slowly by. He was breathing heavily as he struggled to pedal down the street. He didn't look like he'd be capable of taking much of a ride, so I let him go. Then a jock raced by, a skateboard in the basket on the front of his bike. Now there was someone who looked like he knew how to have a good time. I hurried to catch up with him, but he was too quick for me. Just as well, it could have turned into a hell ride.

I waited under the blue sky, buzzed and for the moment free of all bad thoughts. This, I realized, was what staying in the moment meant. True I got to this state with the help of medical marijuana but no matter, I was in a groove. Just then a woman with gorgeous blonde hair glided to the corner. She looked a little like Pam used to look, had the same great smile and pretty blue eyes. She wasn't going too fast, nor too slow. When she slowed at a stop sign, I hopped on. Her aqua beach cruiser had a big seat, and the front basket had colorful plastic flowers pasted on it. This was going to be great. Why hadn't I thought about doing this before?

We cycled down California Avenue toward Palisades Park. After crossing Ocean she turned left and we rode through the park. Being a weekday, it wasn't that crowded. I figured this chick was an out-of-work actress or model, though it seemed like a lot of people didn't work much around here. I felt like I didn't have a care in the world. I couldn't wait to tell Jerry about my new pastime. The three of us could go biking together.

I became somewhat apprehensive as she sped down the steep hill leading to the ocean bike path, holding onto the banana seat for dear life (crazy, I know). But soon we were flying along on the path, passing through Venice Beach like two soaring seagulls enjoying the crisp, clean air. Her long blonde hair floated like silk in the breeze, my scales shimmered and swayed in the sun. When we reached Washington Boulevard her phone rang. She stopped, put both feet on the ground, and reached into the basket for her cell. "Hey, what's up? Where are you?" she said.

I sat on the back of the bike digging the day, as we used to say. I was just along for the ride. Yeah, just along for the ride.

"I know where Jessica lives. I'll be there in a minute." She tossed her phone into the basket, rode up Washington, made a quick turn onto Speedway, and after going a block or so, abruptly hit the brakes. Unprepared for the sudden stop, I lost balance and slipped off. I started to get back on, when she hopped off, locked the bike to a pole, grabbed her cell and walked quickly down the block, where she entered a two-story apartment building.

I was stranded. No way home. I had no idea where the buses ran in this part of town, and to make matters worse, I was suddenly straight. Completely. But I knew somehow I must find my way.

I sat on a garbage can in the alley to ponder my options. I couldn't think straight when I was straight these days, too much stuff rushing into my head. Pam...Harley...Pam and Harley...

Lucky for me a couple of teenage boys walked by laughing like maniacs and smoking an extremely fat joint. I followed them in close pursuit, breathing in the tasty, plentiful and much needed smoke. They lit another. Man, this was turning out to be a good day after all. By the time we reached the wings and pizza stand at the ocean end of Washington Boulevard, I was blitzed. The people around me sat at outdoor tables eating. I was getting hungry, but like years after giving up cigarettes, the urge to eat quickly passed. I watched the bike riders glide on and off the path. Now that I was stoned it dawned on me: I'd hitch a ride home. Brilliant. I picked my target, a twenty-something guy with strong legs, necessary for the headwinds he'd encounter cycling north. While he stopped for a slice, I jumped on the back of his bike.

Soon we were breezing along and I felt no pain. This guy was a good, no-nonsense rider. The sun started going down, but I wasn't worried. I'd make it back before dark. Never cared much for the dark, especially now that I was a spook. Forget the stories Hollywood manufactures, our best stuff is done strictly during daylight hours. We sleep at night just like most of you. At night we have a tendency to bump into stuff and sometimes even knock things over. I suppose that's where the expression "bump in the night" came from. True, some spirits enjoy scaring the shit out of the living particularly when it's dark, but trust me, I wasn't into any of that unless it was absolutely necessary.

We reached the Ferris wheel. Lights in the amusement park went on. I was getting anxious but my ride was still going strong. Until it wasn't. He pulled over to a bike rack, jumped off, and locked his bike. As he was getting off the bike shifted, and I fell to the ground. I stood and straightened my scales, admittedly disoriented. He strode away, not the least bit concerned he'd left me in the lurch.

There were blocks to travel before I was home and some of them were uphill. Fortunately I was still stoned. I flew over the bridge spanning PCH. The sun was perilously close to slipping into the ocean. Soon it would be dark. I hurried along, stopping only a short while to rest on a bench. I vowed to myself to get in better shape but had no idea how. I got up and carefully crossed the street. I'd seen spirits knocked down after getting hit by a car. Of course they were in no danger of dying a second time, but it didn't look like something I'd want to experience.

It was dark when I reached my building. I waited outside for someone to come by to open the glass door. Larry and Greg were on their way out for the night; I staggered past them. I was right near Harley's apartment, lumbering along to the staircase in time to see Pam go inside. At that point I could barely walk and definitely couldn't fly. I couldn't remember ever being this tired. There was no chance of me getting inside Harley's before his door shut. Slow as a garden slug I struggled to the wall of the apartment opposite his, dropped onto the cold cement floor and fell into a dead (no joke intended) sleep.

Chapter 14
NOBODY KNOWS ANYTHING

I woke with the first early morning slamming of the doors. I peered down the hall and saw a guy walking towards the lobby. I was pretty sure he came out of 108. What a jerk, didn't he care that the rest of us were still sleeping?

I felt like shit. I was cold, my back hurt and my scales were twisted. I knew the time had come to lay off the weed. Okay, maybe that was too harsh. Cutting back would work just fine. I got to my feet. I didn't know if Pam was still inside Harley's apartment. I flew up the stairs. Our apartment door was closed, as I expected it would be. I flew around the corner to our balcony. The slider was shut but the blinds were open. Pam walked into the bedroom dressed for work. I rushed back to the front door and waited for her to open it on her way out. As soon as she did, I flew right by her. I hurried into the bedroom to see if she'd left the slider open; she had. Fresh breezes flowed into the bedroom from the ocean; bad thoughts flew into my head. She could have spent the night at Harley's, then come upstairs to get ready for work. The bed was made, circumstantial evidence she hadn't slept in it. Or they both could have been up here, and he could have gone back downstairs earlier, probably to take care of Sam. As I lay passed out in front of his apartment, anything could have transpired and I wouldn't know what. This paranoia was yet more reason to give up the weed.

I lay on the bed. It was too early to do anything else. Even if I wanted to smoke, no one was at the pool and hadn't I just decided to cut back? Too soon to renege. I tossed and turned anxiously and then a miracle occurred; my scales ceased trembling and I fell into a peaceful sleep. I dreamt about Pam, beautiful Pam. It felt like we were really together, not before when we were undergrads at NYU, but now, right now, in Santa Monica somewhere, the sun shining on us, soft breezes blowing.

I woke and sun and ocean air danced through the open slider. I remembered dreaming about being with Pam. I couldn't remember if we were dead or alive. In either case, we were happy. But thoughts of Harley cut short my reverie. I got up and took off from the balcony railing down to his apartment. Jerry and Jen would know what went on last night.

I raced through Harley's open slider. His ugly black and white comforter and red top sheet were bunched together in a disheveled heap atop

178

his bed. The guy never made his bed, but still the sight of this gave me pause. Two pillows with red cases were close together at the head of the bed. Maybe he slept with Sam last night, or maybe he... No, I wouldn't put that into words, not even to myself. I flew into the living room propelled by anxiety. Harley was sitting on the couch eating a bowl of cereal. He wore a pair of blue cotton pajamas, the kind someone buys for you for a hospital stay. He must have quite a collection. Sam was at his side wearing a nurse's uniform. Jerry and Jen sat together on a chair. A soap opera played out dramatically on the big screen TV. A beautiful woman had just sprung back to life surprising the crap out of her cheating husband and her best friend; now that was something I could have written.

"Hey, Henry, what's up?" Jerry said.

"I have to know what's going on with Pam and Harley. Don't lie to me. I need the truth. I know she was here last night."

"Calm down, Henry. Nothing happened, that's what. Pam came over with godmother sandwiches from Bay Cities. Boy I used to be crazy about those. Had to have a side of macaroni salad with it, though. They make one helluva macaroni salad. Just the right amount of mayonnaise." He looked wistful.

"Jerry..."

"Sorry, got sidetracked. They sat on the couch and watched *Little Women: LA*. Ever see that show? Amazing stuff. You think dead people have it rough, you haven't experienced anything until you see what little people go through."

"What the hell are you talking about?"

"Dwarfs, Henry. They used to call them midgets, but that's no longer politically correct. They have all kinds of physical problems and when they have kids they don't know if the kid will be little or average. That's what they call people of normal height. Average. And one of the women got hitched to an average guy who turns out to be a sex addict. He's been sexting online and Briana, that's his little person wife, has the proof. And now she's pregnant. Her friends and family warned her about him, but she didn't listen."

"Jerry, that's all very interesting but in case you haven't noticed, I'm freaking out about Pam. She's been spending a lot of time with Harley and it's hard for me to believe nothing's going on. Jen, I got the impression you thought the same."

"I guess I did, but I was wrong. Jerry and I are here almost every minute they are. And nothing's happened, nothing at all. They're friends, Henry. I'm fairly certain Harley doesn't have the kind of interest in women you think he has. He's more into Sam than any human. Sam and Frogman."

"Frogman?"

"A green rubber frog he keeps on the bathroom sink. The kind children play with when they take baths. He has long conversations with Frogman. Asks his advice, tells him his troubles. Sometimes he sets him up on the couch next to Sam to watch TV. For lack of a more professional diagnosis, Harley's fried. Fried and harmless, Henry. Honestly. Pam's just being nice to him, that's all."

"What can I say? I'm an idiot."

"No, just a man. That's how men think when they're in love. They think other men love the woman they love. But it isn't so, at least not with Pam and Harley."

So as it turned out I'd been driving myself nuts for nothing, a skill I've always excelled at. Pam's a good soul and Harley needed a friend. Now this definitely called for some celebratory weed. "It's a great day. Why sit around here when we can go to the pool?" I said, filled with good cheer and the anticipation of good smoke.

"Anyone out there?" Jerry said.

"Bob from 209. Some chicks too."

"Got some stuff to do. We'll meet you there."

Okay, okay, I couldn't make it through one day. But I'd take only a couple of tokes. Promise.

One toke turned into ten or thereabouts. Tomorrow would be a good day to start cutting back, I rationalized. Today I had too much to celebrate. This left me, no surprise here, sprawled on my back on a pool lounge eavesdropping on two cool-looking chicks talking about their boyfriends. That's what chicks do, right? But complaining would be more like it. Hard to find a woman who's not complaining. Then again, most of us give them plenty to complain about. It's an endless cycle and no one's really to blame. It's just the way things are, once you get past age five or so. I remembered the first female I fell for. It was in Mrs. Taylor's first grade class. Regina Ann Goldberg had the shiniest blonde hair. I was mesmerized by her golden bangs, stared at them for hours. No matter what she did on the monkey bars or swings, her hair swung right back into place. You could say it was her hair I fell for. Everyone in my family, even distant cousins, had plain brown hair. But Regina was cute too. And smart. She read better than anyone in the class. Mrs. Taylor had her read to us more than any of the other kids. That really impressed me. I struggled with reading until I got the hang of it in second grade. I liked to think of Regina as my girlfriend, but truth is she liked another boy in our class. He had the same kind of hair as hers. Whatever. You can move on pretty fast when you're that young.

So I was staring up at the palm fronds whistling in the wind, not a care in the world, when Jennifer came flying out her slider door headed straight for me. She looked grim. I worried something happened to Jerry. She sat at the bottom of my lounge, arms wrapped protectively around herself.

"What's the matter, Jennifer?"

She hesitated. "Oh, Henry." This sounded bad. Something happened to Jerry. But what could happen to him that hadn't happened already?

"Henry, it's Pam." Oh, Jesus, they were wrong about Pam and Harley; the two of them are together. There was nothing to celebrate. I resigned myself to returning to a state of constant anxiety. Pam and Harley, man. I knew it...

"It's not what you're thinking, Henry." My face brightened, my being lightened. I felt stoned again in a good way.

She continued. "There's been an accident. A car accident. Pam was driving on the 10. She's at Saint John's. I'm so sorry, Henry."

I didn't react at first. My thoughts rushed at me in all different directions; it was like getting sacked by a bunch of linebackers. "How do you know?" I finally managed to ask.

"A friend of Pam's called Harley. She was in the car with her. She called everyone in Pam's cell. I don't think she's doing so well. Harley just went to see her."

I wished I hadn't gotten high. It didn't seem right to be getting twisted while your girl was going through a car accident and being rushed to the hospital. "I'm going," I said, getting to my feet.

"We'll go with you." Jerry stood on their patio looking as worried as I'd ever seen him, and that is saying a lot.

We took the bus to the hospital. None of us spoke on the way. We walked inside and went to the Emergency Room. We knew our way around this place like the backs of our scaly hands. We found Pam on top of a gurney, drapes drawn around her cordoned-off area. She was hooked to machines, and the back of her head was wrapped in bandages. The three of us stood paralyzed with fear, when we heard a familiar voice in the hall.

"What do you mean I can't see her. She's my best friend." It' was Harley. I flew out to see what was going on. He was gripping Sam like a life preserver.

"I'm sorry, sir, but it's hospital rules. You must be a member of the family to visit anyone in the ICU." She stared at Sam but made no mention of him/her. Sam wore a motorcycle jacket but no pants. Harley must have been in the middle of dressing the bear when he got the call about Pam.

"I won't leave until I see Pam," he said. Sam was smashed against his chest and plastic-wrapped flowers in need of resuscitation dangled from his free hand.

"Do I have to get someone to escort you out?" the nurse asked, as pleasantly as if she was offering him a sandwich or a cup of tea.

At this he backed off. He'd had enough hospital experience to understand she meant what she said, regardless of her delivery. And with his history he couldn't afford to fool around or he could wind up strapped to a gurney himself. He shuffled off down the hall.

I flew back to Pam, who was oblivious to it all. I knew enough to realize she was in a coma. "I'm staying," I said, planting myself on the green linoleum floor.

"We're with you," Jerry said. And the three of us sat and waited. And waited. And waited. We didn't know if it was morning, afternoon or night. This was not the waiting room in radiation. This was not sunny and comfortable. This was one of Dante's circles of hell.

We had no way of knowing how much time passed. Pam's sister visited often. Nurses and doctors glided in and out of her cubicle. She hadn't moved at all, and yet one nurse, Marianne according to her name tag, talked softly to her and held her hand whenever she was on duty. She carried on whole conversations with Pam, not unlike Harley with Sam and Frogman. One day Marianne left an old transistor radio playing at low volume on Pam's hospital tray. It was tuned to a classic rock station. "I know you can hear this," she said to Pam. Tom Petty was singing "American Girl." "Enjoy," she whispered, going into the hall.

I stood and watched Pam. I could swear she was moving. It wasn't much, almost imperceptible, but I believed she could hear the music. I started talking to her myself. "I'm here with you, Pam. I'll always be with you." I told her whatever came to mind. Just like Marianne, I wouldn't give up hope.

Big Ed came by. "Keep up the good fight, Henry my boy," he said. "She'll come round. You just keep talkin' to her and playing that good old southern rock. She'll turn the corner. Seen it happen plenty."

And one day it did. Jerry and Jen had gone to visit Aunt Irene; no one else was around. I was walking the perimeter of Pam's bed to get some exercise. Would have done some yoga if I could remember any poses just to get the kinks out. My mind entertained a whole bunch of "what ifs," so I wasn't paying close attention to Pam. On my 57th lap (my counting mania had started again), I whirled around the bottom of the gurney and glanced Pam's way to find her staring at me, eyes wide open. I don't think she was actually staring at me, only looking in my direction. But the important thing was her eyes were open. I paced in the hallway waiting for a nurse or doctor to come in to check on her. I felt completely powerless. If only her sister would show up now, or really any live person would do. And finally someone did. Marianne.

"Well, hello Pam. Welcome back," she said smiling, as if it was the most natural thing in the world that Pam abruptly came to. She rang for a doctor. I expected Pam to start talking and being herself, but that didn't happen.

"Can you move your hand?" Marianne asked. Pam didn't respond, but when "LA Woman" started playing on the radio, she smiled. I was blown away.

Slowly Pam made progress, and one day they moved her out of the ICU and upstairs to a private room. It had a big window facing Santa Monica Boulevard. According to the doctors she wasn't out of the woods, but I knew she'd be fine.

That night in her new room, Jerry, Jen and I crumpled together on an upholstered chair by the window. Cars and buses rumbled by two flights below. Pam was still hooked up to a monitor. I watched her and thought about how much I loved her. The hum of slowing traffic sounded like ocean waves to me. I dozed off. I dreamt about Pam. We sat on an old green Mexican blanket spread on the sand. The wind wasn't blowing like it usually does down by the water; it was warm and there was a big blue cloudless sky above us. Looking east over the mountains giant storm clouds gathered. But nothing would happen here, at least not for awhile. The storm was far away. We were safe.

The next morning we visited Aunt Irene and her boyfriend. They were doing well in radiation. We made a pit stop in the cafeteria to tell Ed the good news about Pam. "Told you so," Ed said happily. "I knew she was gonna make it."

We flew back to her new room, stopping cold at the doorway. Pam was surrounded by a flurry of nurses, doctors and a screaming machine. The three of us watched in panic as they attempted to revive her. Sun streamed through the window heedless of the horror taking place. I couldn't understand what went wrong. She was getting better. Just yesterday she was able to move her left hand after Marianne's prompt. And she opened her lips to say something although no words came out. At the time her eyes were wide open and I swear she was looking at me, looking at me and trying to talk. I was desperate to know what she wanted to say. Maybe that she could see me. Yes, that had to be it. She saw me. But now this. I looked on as the medical team tried to ward off what was starting to look inevitable. I was devastated when Marianne covered Pam with the white sheet that had been pushed aside during their efforts.

Everyone left to minister help to those still well enough to receive it. Jerry and Jennifer stayed by my side. The room was silent. I took Pam's hand in mine. "You're everything to me," I said. But her eyes were closed and she didn't move. She was gone, and new worries brewed. Would she come to or was she one of the dead dead? Jerry knew exactly what I was thinking.

"She'll be back," he said.

Jennifer smiled. "For sure. She'll be back before you know it."

Chapter 15
A DAY OF THE DEAD

When the orderly arrived to take Pam to the morgue we followed closely behind. It was far worse knowing what was going to happen; I suppose that's true of most everything. A young woman with better manners than the orderlies I'd had experience with gently deposited her in the cold, dark room. Other corpses lay scattered about. I flew over each to see if anyone had come back. So far none had.

The cold and blackness brought forth a rush of memories and the awful realization that even before I got to the morgue I'd come to and knew exactly what was going on. Yes, everyone is different. Still it worried me that Pam showed no sign of, for lack of a better word, life.

It was too cold for us to stay long, but I was hopeful Pam's sister would send someone for her soon. "How far is the crematorium from here?" I asked Jerry.

"A mile or so."

"I'm going, you know."

"We'll be right there with you."

We were huddled by the light of the computer as if it was giving off heat, when we heard a woman's voice say, "Where am I? Please turn on the lights."

I hoped it was Pam, but it didn't sound like her. Maybe her voice had changed now that she was back from the dead. Jerry flew over to see who was talking. "Not her, Henry," he called out from the far end of the room.

"Who's there?" the woman asked suspiciously.

"I'm Jerry. And who do I have the pleasure of..."

She cut him off. "I don't know any Jerry, except my friend's ex-husband and he moved back to New Jersey. We're not in Jersey, are we?"

"Nope. Santa Monica."

"Thank goodness. So where am I exactly, and why haven't you turned on the lights? The heat too. I'm freezing."

I sat and fretted about Pam, while Jerry, delicate as he could, told Roberta the truth of her whereabouts. It seemed like this woman couldn't stop talking and asking questions, and it was beginning to irritate me. The door opened and an orderly entered. I hoped he came for Pam, but he carted Roberta away. We resumed our vigil for Pam to come to in silence.

Corpses came and corpses went until finally someone arrived to get Pam. Again we followed as she was wheeled down the hall, into the elevator, then along another corridor leading to an exit at the rear of the hospital. The orderly rolled her through the parking lot to a small gray truck with the words "Happy Trails Funeral Home" painted on the side. Now this was a game changer. I had no hands-on experience with buried bodies, though I did meet a few spooks who said they came back that route. One, a guy named Frank, claimed it was no big deal. He first came to when he was six feet under, not a pleasant thought by any means. But according to him, he was able to float to the surface with no hassle at all. He didn't know where he was when he got out, and that was distressing, but lucky for him he ran into another disinterred spirit who'd recently undergone the same fate. He also had been in Saint John's and the pair made their way back to the hospital under the light of a full moon; ultimately they settled in the waiting room of maternity, a happy place. But all that aside, thoughts of Pam stashed beneath the ground were quite unsettling. I for one can't imagine how anyone could push their way out of a casket and through to the ground's surface: we can't fly through anything, making this a colossal undertaking even for the hardiest spirit.

"Remember that guy Frank we met?" Jerry said. I nodded. "He made it out. She's going to be fine, Henry. Just fine."

He wasn't convincing me.

We waited around a couple of days until they had the funeral service. Her sister cried like she'd never stop the entire time. Afterwards, cars lined up behind the large black hearse we hurried into as they loaded Pam into the back. It was hard to believe she was inside this wooden casket. The hearse took off slowly. Jerry, Jen and I sat on three sides of her casket. We passed trees, stores and buildings, having no idea where they were taking her. I worried it would be somewhere in the Valley. I knew there were a lot of cemeteries there. The Valley was one hell of a trip from Santa Monica, particularly in traffic which seemed to get worse all the time. Years ago my ex-wife's cousin was buried there. I refused to accompany Maxine, begged off by inventing an important business meeting that would change our lives in a big way financially. By that time Maxine didn't have much confidence in my ability to make any real money, but she wasn't about to take the chance I was telling the truth so she went to the funeral alone. After she got back I didn't hear the end of it for months: the traffic, the near-miss collisions, the death-defying horror of switching lanes, the oppressive heat, the smog, even bugs, cockroaches as I recall. I'm sure she exaggerated, but she never went back to the Valley, and my not going to that burial became another item on her ever-expanding accounting of grievances against me.

I wished the guy who was driving the hearse would light up a doobie. He looked like a stoner even with his serious black suit and tie on. Now don't get me wrong, it's not like I don't have respect for the dead, especially for the love of my life, but I was freaking out with anxiety and loose-cannon thoughts. For one, if Pam remained a dead dead, how could I visit her in the Valley? It's not like I was able to call Uber. No, I'd have to relocate. Leave Santa Monica for the broiling strip malls and massive freeways of Burbank or Reseda or some other godforsaken burb. It would take getting used to, this move. I knew some people loved the Valley, great shopping, excellent sushi, whatever. I resigned to somehow make the move there work. What kind of guy would I be if I didn't?

To counteract flipping out, I started counting trees we passed. I was at fifty-one when the hearse came to a sudden stop. Doors opened and carefully the driver and his helper slid Pam's box onto a large wooden dolly. Car doors slammed and mourners got in line behind the casket. I realized we hadn't driven on any freeways, and it wasn't hot or smoggy. In fact, faint ocean breezes blew, rustling my scales. I looked around and realized we were at Woodlawn Cemetery on 14th Street. I'd passed by there maybe a thousand times on the way to Ocean Park and Venice. It wasn't as scenic or famous as Westwood Village Memorial Park where Marilyn and Truman were, but it had its own brand of bucolic.

We followed the stream of people over to a freshly dug plot near a tall and stately palm. There was a small commotion as someone approached in the distance screaming, "Don't start yet. Don't do it. Wait for me. Traffic through Santa Monica was murder. Wait. Please." And Harley came towards us taking lunatic strides.

"A friend of my sister's," Pam's sister murmured, clearly hoping no one heard her.

Harley joined the group gathered around the box as it was lowered into the ground. Several mourners gave short speeches, as people took turns throwing dirt on top of the casket. Pam's sister, Harley and a few others cried. Harley held Sam, dressed in black, by one leg as he added a few handfuls of dirt to the pile. My head was to the ground at the edge of the hole; I listened intently to hear Pam speak. Dirt landed all over me, but I continued straining to hear Pam's voice journeying back from the dead.

Jerry came over as people began to leave. "Want to hitch a ride back?"

"Nah, I'm going to stay awhile. You and Jen should go with Harley."

"Sure you don't mind?"

"I could use some time, just the two of us. I have a good feeling about today. With all this jostling around, I think there's a chance she'll come to. I can always take the bus home part of the way. Don't worry about me. I'll be back before it's dark."

"Are you sure?" Jens asked.

I nodded my head and smiled, certain that at any minute I'd hear Pam's voice.

Chapter 16
FULL MOON RISINGS

I sat on the grass by Pam's grave waiting for her to talk. She was near the back end of the burial grounds on the left side; not many people passed by this way. I could tell it was getting late by the angle of the sun and the fact that the air had grown chilly. I knew I should be on my way home but couldn't bring myself to leave her. I thought about the good times we had when we were young. I thought about how I royally screwed everything up. I thought about the years we weren't together because of me. I thought about how we ended up in the same apartment. A chick would say it was our destiny to be together. That sounded touchy-feely to me, and I was never that kind of guy. But I needed her to come back to me now; I considered staying frozen to this spot until she did.

I must have dozed off because when I looked up the sky was dark, and a large bright full moon hung over the city. This place looked like a stereotypical black and white book cover of a haunted cemetery. Given this setting I had several troubles brewing: the first was I didn't want to leave Pam here; the second that it was too dark for me to find my way home; third was that buses didn't run as often this time of night; and fourth that I was scared shitless, plain and simple.

I was sitting on the ground biting the scales on the tips of my fingers when I saw a good-sized silvery, luminescent object headed my way. Holy mother, now what the hell could this be? No longer any question about it, this freaking place was haunted. But why should that bother me when I was an intrinsic part of the haunting? Unfortunately, rational thinking doesn't help me, never usually did. That silvery blob continued floating towards me, still too far for me to make out what it was. I was seriously considering making a run for it when the blob, now too close for comfort, said, "Hello." Turned out to be a woman flyer who looked too young to be on my side of the pond.

"Just hanging out or are you visiting someone?" she asked, landing with a tinkling sound near my feet. This brought Tinker Bell to mind, but this young woman was of regular size, average if you were judging from a little person's perspective. And naturally, she was covered with scales, extra silvery, sparkling scales. The young always had better looking scales.

"My girl. They buried her today," and I pointed to the freshly dug grave. "Pam."

"I'm here for my boyfriend. I come here a lot and every full moon for sure. Lots of spirits drop by then. Makes it kind of a party, like the old days. Timothy and I loved to party. You'll see. They'll be here soon. I'm Summer." Clearly she was of Woodstock generation parents. Man, I had the album and I'd seen the movie countless times, but to this day I regret not going to Woodstock. Probably had a hot date who wasn't into camping.

"Henry, " I said, my face a scaly mess of grief.

"I can see you're very sad, Henry."

"I'm worried Pam won't come back."

"I know exactly how you feel. That's what happened with Timothy."

"You mean he didn't..."

"Never made it back, but I haven't given up hope. If someone's going to come to, it's likely to happen during a full moon. It's an energy thing, the extra pull of gravity and such."

"Do you ever worry that he did come back, but went somewhere else because he didn't know where to find you?"

"The thought occurred to me, but we were living in the same apartment on Ocean Park Boulevard for years. He'd know where to go. Nope, he's still down there," and she patted the ground. "We can't all come back, you know."

"That's what worries me."

By then an army of silvery spooks were swooping over the graves, stopping to talk to one another, then moving on. It was a spectacular sight, and now that Summer was here I wasn't afraid.

But I spoke too soon, because out of seemingly nowhere along came Harley, bounding towards us holding a Trader Joe's shopping bag and a shovel. He was followed closely by the guy who helped him move into our building.

"She's right here, Tony," Harley said, setting the shopping bag down gently inches from where Summer and I sat. Tony carried a shovel in one hand and a flashlight in the other.

"Don't think we'll be needing the light. The moon's shining on her grave. Better get started. No dilly dallying, no farting around." Harley laughed maniacally; Tony joined in with equal mania. They sounded crazy loud in the dead silent cemetery. No other visitors except spirits were around now. They started to dig.

"Jesus, what the hell are these two imbeciles doing?"

"They're digging up Pam's grave, Henry."

"What the hell for?"

"I've seen it happen. As far as I can tell, everyone has a different reason. Love, hate, grabbing a piece or two of buried jewelry or clothing, dropping off a gift of some kind, one final revenge or a last kiss. One time I witnessed a body snatch. No way of knowing what compels someone to do that. I'm pretty certain it was a woman the guy retrieved. Maybe he knew her, maybe he didn't. Most diggers are pretty nuts. The body snatcher I saw looked perfectly normal; shows how you never know about people. When I was still alive it never occurred to me to do that, and I missed Timothy like mad."

"What happened to him?"

"Oxy. Same as me. It was three New Year's Eves ago for Tim; I hit the skids the following New Year. Big party, big heart ache, big drugs."

"Wow, sorry."

"I stick with weed now. Not like I have a choice, but it's cool. Should have done that a long time ago. Timothy, too."

We watched Harley and Tony alternate between digging and sharing a joint. A couple of times we moved to avoid getting hit with flying dirt.

"Land ho," Harley said, standing tall atop Pam's casket like Columbus coming upon America. He thrust his shovel skyward, a joint between his lips. Dirt fell onto his hair and face, but he paid it no mind. He passed the joint up to Tony, who was leaning over grave's edge, then tapped the box with the tip of his shovel and shouted, "Ain't it grand!"

"Do you think he's planning to snatch Pam?" I asked, horrified by the prospect.

"No way. See the bag? I think he's bringing her something. Maybe something to remember him by. One of his scarves or an old sweater he wore a lot. Were they friends?"

"Yeah, I guess. He was a neighbor. She felt sorry for him. The guy's a lunatic."

"I noticed." Summer smiled.

"I thought something was going on between them, but I was wrong."

"He looks a little like the actor in that old *Bonnie and Clyde* movie. Get ready to make a move, Henry. He's about to open the casket. I'll give you some space."

I was standing on the rim of the grave now. Harley was six feet down tugging on the lid of the box. "Man, is this thing locked or what?"

"They don't lock that shit, Trip. It's just stuck. Keep trying."

Finally it opened. "Bring me that bag, will you? Don't throw it. Hand it to me."

"There's probably something breakable inside," Summer said.

Wasting no time, I flew into the coffin hovering face-to-face over Pam. She still looked so beautiful. I thought about staying there with her, just lying down beside her and waiting for Harley to close the lid. I mean, why the hell not? But then I heard something. Only one word. It sounded like "Henry." I looked up at Summer and heard it again. "Henry." But it wasn't coming from Summer.

"Did you hear that, Henry? I think she's back," Summer said excitedly.

I looked down at Pam. Her face and body were dead still in the light of the moon. "Henry, I'm here. I can see you." Her lips weren't moving, but it was definitely Pam talking.

"I saw you. At the hospital, Henry. You were speaking to me. I wanted to tell you so many things. I tried but couldn't get any words out."

And under the moonlit night with Summer, Harley and Tony standing nearby, Pam morphed into a silver scaled outline of herself, and took flight above her dead body. Together we flew up and out of the grave, landing next to Summer.

"Welcome back, Pam," Summer said.

I took Pam's hand in mine. She smiled that same old great smile. "I don't know what's going on or even where I am, but I'm so happy to be with you, Henry," she said.

Harley pulled a bear out of the grocery sack. It looked like Sam only it was cream colored, not brown. It had a pink bow around its neck and wore a pink and green flowered dress. With considerable care he placed the bear onto Pam's chest and positioned one of Pam's arms to encircle it. "Say hello to Harriett," he said to

Pam's dead body, proudly patting the bear's leg. "You'll never be alone now." I saw a few tears trickle down his cheeks.

He closed the casket, leapt up from the grave, and began shoveling dirt back on top. "Give me a hand, Tony. Don't want to land in the clinker for grave digging."

"Or back at Pleasant Hills," Tony said, grabbing his shovel. "Dr. Epstein would not think this is cool."

The mention of Dr. Epstein's name alarmed Harley. He swiveled his head around to see if anyone was watching. A multitude of spooks actually were; stuff like this didn't happen all that often at Woodlawn, not even during a full moon. But although Harley's eyes continued to rove the grounds as he worked, all he saw were graves and trees and a big old moon.

Chapter 17
NO VAMPIRES OR
WEREWOLVES HERE

After saying good-bye to Summer, Pam and I followed Harley and Tony out of the cemetery to Harley's parked car on the street. He opened the door.

"Hurry, Pam," I said, leading her to the backseat atop papers, food and drink containers (empty and partially filled), clothing and run-of-the-mill trash. It was odd that he kept his apartment clean and his car looked like a junkyard.

Pam and I sat close together holding hands. "Can they hear us when we talk?" she whispered.

"Not a word."

"You were in my apartment the whole time?"

"Since the day Maxine chucked my urn at you. I went out a lot during the day, but slept in my urn every single night, except for one time when I got locked out."

"Incredible. I never heard you, never noticed anything out of the ordinary. Nothing like how I would expect it to be with a ghost around. That's what we are, right?"

"Yeah. Not so bad, huh?"

"No," she smiled, crinkling the scales on her nose. "Not so bad. But on some level I must have known you were there because I talked to you a lot."

I smiled. "Yeah, I liked that."

"And I dreamt about you. The dreams were so real I thought you were actually with me."

"I was."

"You can do that?"

"We all can. Well, not every time we try, but sometimes it works."

"So much to contemplate," she said, a dreamy look on her still-pretty face.

"You'll get used to it. It's a new way of life only we're..."

"Dead," she said, filling in the blank. "Can't be politically correct about death. Either you are or you aren't. Anyway, I know all about it. I watched while it happened to me in the hospital. Even in the ambulance I knew everything that was going on. When I was in a coma and you talked to me, I heard every word you said. That nurse, too. At first I thought I might already be dead because she was like an angel and you had shiny scales all over."

"I knew you could hear me, I always believed that. But she was the one who started talking to you. I followed her lead. And she brought you the radio."

"I know. I loved the music."

"Damn," Harley said, turning the key in the ignition again and again. "I was supposed to bring old Mary in, but then Pam had the accident."

"Who's Mary?" Tony asked, lighting a joint.

"My car, numb nut."

Following several more tries, the engine kicked in and we took off down 14th Street. We drove no more than a block when Harley whispered, "Someone's following us." He'd been staring intently in the rearview mirror, but now turned round and looked out the back window.

"Watch out!" Tony screamed.

Harley flipped back in time to avoid side-swiping several parked cars. He laughed. "Nothing like a near-miss to get the adrenaline flowing. Better keep a look-out, Tony, so I can concentrate on driving."

"What am I looking for?"

"Someone following us. Somebody must have seen us digging up Pam's grave. We could be in deep shit."

"Are they jogging or in a car?"

"In a car. Mary's slow now, but even so a jogger could never keep up. Check out that car behind us. The big SUV. Must be undercover cops. Or maybe it's," and his tone turned extra ominous, "Epstein. Keep your eyes peeled. Don't let that car out of your sight."

"Right, boss."

"I'll throw them off the track by turning up random streets."

"Good thinking, Trip."

Harley lurched down one street and up another, zig-zagging his way through Santa Monica. The SUV continued on 14th Street, but this didn't deter Harley from jerk driving the surrounding streets.

"I don't see that car anymore. Haven't for blocks," Tony said.

"Threw them off the track," Harley said. "I'm really good at that. Like Steve McQueen."

"Are you afraid? Being in a car again?" I asked Pam. "Especially this one."

"I'm okay. I'm with you."

"I love you, you know. Always have."

"I love you, too, Henry."

"I've got the munchies," Harley said. "Let's go to Jack's."

"You're a mind reader, Trip," Tony said.

"I wish we could eat," Pam said.

"You'll get used to it."

Harley pulled off Lincoln Boulevard and into a Jack in the Box drive-through. "Four cheeseburgers, two chicken sandwiches, two large curly fries and two big Cokes. Sound like I have it covered, Tony?"

"The makings of a true gourmet meal."

"Don't forget the ketchup please. Lots and lots of those ketchup packets," Harley said into the monitor, finishing the order.

On the way home Harley underwent a fresh bout of paranoia, taking us on an unusually long ride to 4th Street. "Epstein," he mumbled at short intervals. Finally we pulled into the garage. "Stay here," he said to Tony.

Quickly he sprinted out and scrutinized the quiet, well-lit and, except for us, deserted area. He checked underneath a number of parked cars and opened the door where the dumpsters were kept. After sticking his head into both dumpsters, he waved at Tony, indicating it was safe to get out of the car.

"Don't worry, Trip, he's not here. You were too sly for him," Tony grabbed the food and opened the door. We used this opportunity to zip out, then followed them up to the first floor.

Pam took her time floating up the staircase. "Never could do this before," she said laughing.

"Should we try to get into your apartment? You left the slider open," I said.

"Let's," and we soared hand-in-hand to the second floor. We flew down the hallway and rounded the corner, but Pam skidded to a stop, suddenly afraid. It was necessary to fly over to the balcony from the outside hallway, a short trip but two stories up. "I can't do it, Henry."

"I forgot all about that. It took me awhile to get used to the height, too. Don't worry, it just takes practice. We'll go to Harley's. His slider's probably open."

When we got inside, Harley and Tony were eating in the dinette. Jerry and Jennifer sat on the couch in the living room watching television. Harley usually left the TV on for Sam, even when he went out. An old Steve McQueen movie was on. I think it was "Bullitt."

"Wow, you came back!" Jerry said, grinning.

"I knew you would," Jennifer said. "You look beautiful. And like one of us now."

"I haven't seen myself in a mirror yet. I think I'll wait for that."

"You wouldn't believe what happened at the cemetery," I said. "Harley was there."

"No way."

"It's a long story, but he helped get Pam back. I'll tell you about it tomorrow. Where can we crash?"

"I have the perfect spot for you honeymooners," Jen said. "Follow me."

We flew into the dinette, and Jen pointed to an orange bong not far from their blue one. "I can vouch for the fact that it's super comfortable and roomy enough for two. I've never seen Harley use it so you have nothing to worry about. He likes the green one. See you in the morning," and she flew back into the living room.

Pam looked at me like I'd lost my mind. "We can't fit inside that."

"Watch me, then do exactly what I do." I flew up to the shelf, hovered over the bong, dipped one scaly finger inside, then vaporized into the container.

"I can't do that." Pam sounded worried.

"Try."

She took a deep breath and floated gracefully up to the bong, tentatively dipped in her index finger, and vaporized inside the bong.

"Easy, right?"

"Will we be able to get out?"

"Does a leopard have spots?"

"You always used to say that."

* * *

A few days after Pam's funeral, we were all at Harley's. Pam was getting acclimated to death and the five of us (six if you count Sam) were living like we were at a commune in the sixties or seventies. Never did that scene, but always thought it would be very, very cool, Manson and his followers aside. The other day

Jerry came up with the idea of inviting more spooks to move in with us. Sounded like an excellent plan to me. The potheads would have a field day here with Harley around, and the non-imbibers were certainly welcome to join our family. No passing judgment on straight spirits in this apartment. For now Pam's the only one of us lacking stoner interest. Yes, Sam smokes, no lie, and I had to admit since Pam was back I didn't get ripped as often as I used to.

So we were sitting around after flying home from a great afternoon riding the Ferris wheel on the pier (talk about views!), taking a breather before heading to the pool (it's Friday). Harley was out seeing his shrink, and Sam was watching Ellen DeGeneres. She had some author on talking up his new book about vampires and werewolves. I never heard of the guy, but he was making mega bucks writing about this stuff, which sounded pretty ridiculous to me. Werewolves, vampires, witches, zombies, demons and lots of blood sucking. Who would be interested in stories like that?

Ellen held up his latest book, grinning from ear to ear and went on about how much she and Portia enjoyed reading *Vampires Rule My World*. Could anyone have come up with a worse title? Sounded like something Harley would dream up. And who were all these people buying his books? I could have written about vampires and werewolves, I'm sure I could have. But I for one can't write about things that don't happen. Never was much for the fantasy world, in print or on screen. But just like I was wrong thinking Starbucks stocks were for suckers when they first came out, there was a big market for vampires and werewolves. It's not for me, though; I refused to sell out, not even now. I would stick to what I or someone I knew had actually experienced. Slice of life stuff. Stories like this.

Oh, and one more thing I should come clean with. It's about that destiny shit. You know, how most chicks would say Pam and I being together was our destiny. Well, okay, it was true. It was our destiny to be together. There, I've said it, touchy-feely as it may be.

I have to go now. We're all going to the pool. Larry and Greg are there, and Harley just came back from getting his head shrunk with a bag of medical and a new bong he picked up on his way home. Maybe I'll see you around one of these days. No worries. Things on this side are pretty cool. And if you can find your way to Santa Monica I'll be happy to show you the ropes, maybe even find you a bong to stay in. We'll consider all comers. It'll be a blast. Admit it, haven't you always wanted to move into *Melrose Place*?

Later, man.

THE END